PHJC

J

When Kids Drive
Kids Crazy

EDA LeSHAN

When Kids Drive Kids Crazy

*How to Get Along With Your
Friends and Enemies*

DIAL BOOKS FOR YOUNG READERS
NEW YORK

Published by Dial Books for Young Readers
A Division of Penguin Books USA Inc.
375 Hudson Street
New York, New York 10014

Design by Ann Finnell
Printed in the U.S.A.
First Edition
E
1 3 5 7 9 10 8 6 4 2
Library of Congress Cataloging in Publication Data
LeShan, Eda J.
When kids drive kids crazy / by Eda LeShan.
p. cm.
Summary: Discusses why some young people are brats, bullies,
or otherwise hurtful to others and how to cope with them,
help them, and develop good friendships.
ISBN 0-8037-0866-1 :
1. Aggressiveness (Psychology) in children—Juvenile literature.
2. Aggressiveness (Psychology) in adolescence—Juvenile literature.
3. Interpersonal conflict in children—Juvenile literature.
4. Interpersonal conflict in adolescence—Juvenile literature.
5. Childhood friendship—Juvenile literature.
6. Friendship in adolescence—Juvenile literature.
[1. Interpersonal relations.]   I. Title.
BF723.A35L47 1990 90-32091 CIP AC
155.4'18232—dc20

For my granddaughter, Rhiannon Jackson,
who gave me suggestions for this book and whom
I love more than any other "kid"

CONTENTS

Introduction

There is no doubt that people "drive each other crazy"—in fact sometimes we drive ourselves crazy. But that word *crazy* has different meanings, and I want to explain what it means to me.

A few years ago I wrote a book called *When Your Child Drives You Crazy*. I met an eight-year-old boy who told me that title made him angry. It sounded as if I didn't like children. I explained that what I had meant was that children drive parents crazy when the parents don't understand their children—when they can't figure out how a child is feeling or what to do about it. Michael said that was okay. Then he suggested that grownups drive children crazy when children don't understand grownups, and I thought his suggestion was so excellent that I wrote a book called *When Grownups Drive You Crazy.*

When that book was published I went to talk about it to some fifth-grade classes in New Jersey. Many of the children wrote me letters as part of a class assignment after the meeting, and one fifth grader named Krisi Tadych wrote, "I liked your presentation but I think you should write a book called *When Kids Drive Kids Crazy.*" I thought that was a wonderful idea. I remember very well how I felt when I was growing up and someone made fun of me, or a friend deserted me, or I felt very unpopular.

Now that I am a grownup I can understand why kids can be mean to each other, why they can drive each other crazy. It's when they don't understand each other or even themselves. I think growing up would have been a little easier for me if I had understood more about children's feelings when I was young, and I hope this book will help you.

1

When Do Kids Drive Kids Crazy?

When I stand and watch children in a park playground or in a school recess period outdoors, it doesn't matter whether the children are three or seven or nine or eleven years old. Sooner or later I will see two children fighting. In a nursery-school group one child might pinch another child as a way to try to get a wagon the other child is using. In a group of fourth graders I might see several children ganging up on one child, and sometimes several children will be punching each other— maybe even throwing stones at each other. If I'm lucky, watching young people in junior and senior high school, I will see that when they get angry they fight with words, but on unlucky days

I may see very frightening things, even children using knives. Are all children natural enemies? Are we born wanting everything for ourselves so that we get angry at any other child who seems to have something we want? There is surely no question that from the earliest years brothers and sisters can feel angry at and jealous of each other, each one feeling they are not loved equally or treated fairly by their parents. Is that the whole story? Do all children feel like rivals, enemies?

Most certainly not. In those same playgrounds and school yards I see many other things happening. I see a four-year-old comforting another child who has fallen and hurt her knee; I see two first graders working out a way to take turns on a bicycle. I see groups of children running, laughing, playing games, making up imaginary stories and acting them out. I see children with their arms around each other.

I know two things. I know that the way children treat each other has a lot to do with how old they are. The second thing I know is that whether or not children can learn to be better friends depends a lot on whether or not grownups help them to learn about themselves and each other.

I don't believe that children—or grownups— are natural enemies. I believe that everyone wants to feel loved and that when we feel our parents love us, we can begin to learn how to give love to others. I think we all want friends. But the younger a child is, the harder it may be to work things out in a friendly way.

If you watch a group of two-year-olds playing in a sandbox, sooner or later you will probably hear some screaming and see some scratching and biting. The reason is that little children want what they want when they want it—right away—and they haven't yet learned any other ways to show how they feel.

On your way to the school bus you probably see a couple of boys playfully wrestling; perhaps one of them took an apple from the other; maybe they want to show off in front of some girls they are watching. Maybe they are just full of energy because they have been sitting too much all day. You might see a girl teasing a boy because she got a higher mark on a math quiz. It used to be that girls were taught to be quiet and submissive and "ladylike." Now we know girls have as much right to compete as boys. Competition becomes very important to school-age children, whether in the classroom or the playing field. By that time many grownups have shown children that they feel grades are very important, and winning—being the best—is the most important goal.

And if you have any teenage brothers or sis-

ters—or if you are approaching that age yourself—you know that adolescence is, in some ways,
the worst time of all. Young people are desperate
to be popular, to be like everyone else, not to be
different or to stand out. Adolescents are taking
important steps out into the world, away from the
safety of their families, and it is frightening, but
necessary in order to become an adult.

What this book is going to be about is why
kids behave differently as they are growing up and
which kinds of things help them to enjoy each
other instead of driving each other crazy.

A school bus stops to pick up eight-year-old
Debbie who has just moved into the neighborhood, and this is her first day at her new school.
A tall, skinny boy in the back of the bus yells at
her, "Well, look at the new fatso!" Most of the
children around him laugh. Debbie is tall and
chubby and very self-conscious about her size. John
continues tormenting her—a week or two later he
shouts that she's the dumbest kid in the class.
The school that Debbie went to before she was
transferred had a different third-grade program,
and she is confused. She goes home crying almost
every day.

Why is John tormenting her, and why are some
of the others encouraging him? On the school bus
John has found a "random target" for a lot of an-

ger. A random target is someone who we feel is weaker, more vulnerable, than we are, and whom we attack when we are really mad at somebody else but are afraid of that person finding out how angry we feel. John's father is an alcoholic. When he drinks, he gets very mean and often hits John and his mother. John is scared to death of his father and angry at his behavior and he's also angry at his mother for not protecting him enough.

When Debbie gets on the bus, John can see at once that she feels shy and afraid and worried about whether or not she will make friends. She becomes an easy target for his angry, painful feelings about himself and his family. In this case Debbie's mother suggested that Debbie invite John over to play some afternoon after school. John was very surprised. Debbie has a great big shaggy dog, and the dog jumped all over John and licked his face. "He likes me!" John said. Debbie's mother told John he could come over some Saturday, if he wanted to, when the family usually went on a picnic. Once you get to know someone and like that person, you don't want to hurt him or her. As John had a chance to get some relief from his home situation, he wanted to grow up to be like Debbie's father. The more John talked, the more Debbie's family felt that somebody ought to know about John's hard times at home. They talked about him to the guidance counselor who helped John's mother to go to some meetings of Al-Anon, an organization that helps families where there is an alcoholic. It's never easy to solve serious problems, but unhappiness at home is one of the reasons a kid may drive other kids crazy.

Twelve-year-old Shana screams at her seven-year-old brother that he has to stay in his room or go to a friend's house during her birthday party because he's "a disgusting slob." Does she hate her brother? Probably not. But at twelve very little matters more than trying to appear to be perfect, to be exactly the same as all her girlfriends. It is a time of life when most young people feel very unsure of themselves and want more than anything else to be popular.

Shana's mother is angry at first—she can see that Shana has hurt Charlie's feelings, but then she remembers how she felt when she was Shana's age. She tells Charlie that it would be a good time to go to the roller skating rink with some of his friends, and she arranges for another parent to take them. She knows from her own experience that when she got older and no longer felt so insecure, she didn't care at all how her brother looked.

Josh, in fourth grade, is not very tall for his age and not as strong as the class bully who always waits for him outside the school. David knocks Josh's books out of his hands and throws them in a puddle or the dirty snow. David laughs out loud to see Josh frightened and miserable. David makes sure other kids are watching. They are afraid of him and so they laugh, even though they feel very uncomfortable. Josh is one of the smartest kids in his class. His mother is a lawyer and his father is an architect. He lives in a pretty fancy house and has a very expensive bike.

David is having a lot of trouble with reading and math. His parents punish him all the time for his poor grades. Neither of his parents went to college. His mother stays home taking care of five other children, and his father works in a factory and is sometimes laid off, and then they go on welfare and have to get food stamps. The truth is that David is so jealous of Josh he just can't stand it. For the moment that he is making Josh miserable and other kids are paying attention to him, he feels popular and successful, but that feeling doesn't last very long.

Any one of several things might happen in such a situation. If David keeps on beating up Josh, his parents might report it to the school. If the principal tells David's parents, he will be in more trouble than ever. Maybe Josh could get so mad that he'd try to fight back, even if he lost. The other kids might respect him for trying, even if he got a bloody nose and a black eye; finally they would have the courage to turn away from David and let him know they did not admire him at all.

Can you think of something Josh might do that might be a better solution? Josh knows that David is not doing well in school. One day he might pick up his wet books and tell David he needs to talk to him, privately. David is too surprised to say no. As they walk alone, Josh might say, "Listen, if you want to, you could come to my house a couple of days a week after school and I could help you with your homework."

This would be the hardest thing to do. It would take a lot of courage on Josh's part and David would be caught between trying to maintain his tough attitude and admitting he needs help. It's not easy choosing—finding—ways to solve problems between kids, but it is possible. The truth is that young people, whether in grade school or junior high school, all recognize such situations, and whether they are the ones causing trouble or are the victims, nobody is really happy about such experiences. If we can begin to understand the cause of such behavior, we are taking the first step toward solving these kinds of problems. If we ask ourselves *when* there are likely to be such difficult relationships, we may find the key to changing things around.

The children whose feelings are being hurt or the children who can't fight back feel awful when such things happen; the children who do the hurting or the fighting have, almost always, been hurting in their own feelings long beforehand. The meanest child, laughing the hardest, may well be much more unhappy than the child he or she is being mean to.

When kids drive other kids crazy it's no fun for anyone. Some teasing and fighting is just a natural part of being young, but sometimes—maybe a lot of the time—it gets to be just too much. It helps if we understand just what is going on. It's not a simple problem because all of us have complicated and mixed-up feelings, both children and grownups.

When kids drive other kids crazy it's usually when there are *feelings* that nobody is recognizing or talking about. A toddler bites another little kid because he *feels* frustrated and doesn't know any better way to express his feelings. A second grader teases a friend about having "an ugly dress," when she is *feeling* jealous. A five-year-old is yelled at by his father for "playing too rough" with a baby sister. The five-year-old is scared to death of some of the thoughts he is having, wishing the baby had never been born because he *feels* he has lost his parents' love. He feels guilty and fright-

ened and he finds little ways of showing he's unhappy.

Selma is crying hysterically, screaming at her
mother that she is *not* going to school and there
is nothing her mother can do about it. Selma says
she will run away. She says her mother hates her.
She takes a pair of shoes and throws them at the
wall. Her mother is so mad she's afraid she's going
to hit Selma so she leaves the room, slamming the
door hard. An unusual before-breakfast scene on a
school day? Not at all! I'll bet you can think of
days like that. Selma happens to be eleven. There
is some problem about the way her feet are growing, and it is necessary for her to wear corrective
shoes for a year or so. Selma says she would rather
die.

When such episodes occur it is because of "peer
pressure." It means that this is a time of life when
a young person is absolutely desperate to be popular. The idea of being different is unbearable.
Selma feels she will be left all alone, that nobody
will want to have anything to do with her, that
her friends will whisper that she's a freak. It's not
likely that she can put all these feelings into words,
and she is certain there is *no way* she can possibly
live with this problem.

But there is another side to the *when* of behavior. There are just as important reasons when kids

are wonderful to each other! The fourth day of school a schoolmate came up to Debbie and said, "I would like to be your friend." Shana may not have wanted her brother to come to a party, but when he got pneumonia and was so sick, and the doctor took him to the hospital, Shana was so scared and worried that she couldn't sleep. After David began doing better at school, he told his father he would try to get jobs shoveling snow in winter and cutting grass in the summer to help earn money for the family, and one day he bought Josh a beautiful compass as a present. Selma decided to make fun of herself. When she got to her classroom, she said, "Okay, everybody, laugh all you want—my shoes make me look like Pinocchio!" Three girls bared their teeth and one said, "And how about us looking like we've got barbed-wire fences in our mouths?"

The same kid that bit another child probably wants to hug and kiss this "friend" the next day when they are happily painting pictures next to each other.

What's this all about? The times and places when things go well and when they don't?

When young people feel angry, threatened, insecure, shy, ashamed, jealous, frightened, and/or unloved—that's when there are problems. When parents insist that you make friends with relatives or with the neighbors' children, it can be very frustrating and annoying and often interferes with friendly feelings, but when a young person feels good about him- or herself, those are the moments when we become most loving and giving to others. I don't believe anyone is born wanting to be mean or hateful. Quite the contrary. I think human beings are born with the potential for becoming loving, caring human beings who will value friendship above all else. Friendship—whether between brothers and sisters, or parents and children, or schoolmates, or teachers and students, or married couples. In fact all people in all countries of the world feel a deep hunger for being close. Some things interfere. Some things are just part of being young and inexperienced. Whenever we have good times or hard times we need to see what's happening and then we need to try to figure out *why* some things are happening. Once we figure out the *when* and the *why,* we are well on the way to becoming the kind of human beings that can help to make the world around us a safer and friendlier place in which to live.

2

Why Do Kids Drive Kids Crazy?

Children aren't born knowing how to get along with each other. At first, babies want the full and undivided attention of grownups and are not interested in other children, unless a much older brother or sister takes care of them.

Sometime during the first year or so children begin to notice other children. Sixteen-month-old Maryann starts screaming when her mother puts her in a playpen so she can read a story without interruption to Maryann's five-year-old sister. Maryann sees her sister as an imposter who is daring to take some attention away from her. Young children begin to notice other children their own age, and are fascinated by children who are older.

Often there is a kind of hero worship of an older child who can do so many things and be so entertaining and caring. Babies and very young children are pretty helpless, but as they get older, they begin to see other children as competitors and rivals. Children become jealous of each other and worry about getting enough love and attention from grownups; they worry about other children taking away their toys. At the same time, they begin to realize that you can often have much more fun with other children than with adults— it is exciting, you feel curious, you want to *play*.

A main characteristic of all human beings of all ages is having mixed feelings, and this is surely true when children feel both threatened and delighted by the presence of other children.

At two and three years of age children have not yet learned about how to get along with each other. Ways of defending themselves usually include refusing to take turns, biting, hitting, scratching, screaming, pinching, taking things away from others, and running to a nearby grownup for protection when things get too rough. Young children don't have enough experience or language ability or information to know any other ways to assert themselves. And yet, at the very same time they want to be with other children because they want to play.

No matter how often children may get angry at each other, there are many reasons why they will find ways to be friends. One of the most important reasons is that children know how to play. No matter how much grownups may try to join in a "tea party" or a puppet show or any other activities that call for imagination, they never really get totally involved the way children can.

When I was a child, I had a friend named Janice. We both loved playing with dolls, until we were about eleven or twelve years old. (Children grew up *much* more slowly when I was a child!) Now, looking back, I know we *believed* in our make-believe. It was so real, the feeling that we were mothers taking care of our babies. We were totally absorbed, involved, carried into a special fantasyland realer than real.

I had another friend, Elaine. She lived in a house on a lake and her family owned a canoe. There was a small island in the middle of the lake and we paddled the canoe there, where we pretended to be lost at sea on a tropical island. I remember that stones were meat and weeds were vegetables—and for those hours together, we believed that our game was real. Now I marvel at our imagination, and envy children who can easily move in and out of different worlds, different realities. This is a very precious gift that children give to each other—so special, in fact, that often it seems as if no adult can ever understand. They are right. Most of us lose much of that power of pretending. It surely is a talent that draws children to each other. When children pretend to be fire fighters, police officers, mothers or fathers, bus drivers, cowboys, or astronauts, it feels realer than real.

Despite all the reasons children enjoy being together, by the time children get to elementary school and junior high, there may still be quite a bit of physical fighting, but the big change is that now children have much more ease with language—they can communicate with words. Michael tells Jeff, "Let's be best friends." Or Melinda tells Jason, "If you don't stop pushing me I'm going to tell the teacher." Katie tells Rachel, "Ellen is a pig and a snob—let's not let her into our secret club."

Now children can express love and rivalry, anger, all the kinds of feelings we all have, but more often now it is in words.

What I remember best about being in elementary school is that sometimes it felt like a jungle of wild beasts, and sometimes it was the happiest place to have fun, and sometimes there was meanness, and other times there was so much love.

In third grade there was a girl named Emily who either had some kind of bladder trouble or was very frightened and anxious. Once in a while she wet her pants, and we were horrible to her, teasing and laughing. Sixty years later, I still feel ashamed! But every child in that class was probably scared to death of something like that happening to them, and each of us wanted to be popular, so we ganged up on someone who was more helpless than we felt about ourselves. There was also a girl named Marian who was terribly shy and blushed easily. We loved to do things that would make her blush even though we knew we made her miserable.

On the other hand, there was a boy named Robert who was very quiet and kind to everyone. He was very pale and didn't ever have to take gym. After he had been absent for several weeks, our teacher told us he had a very serious heart problem—and was very sick. He had been born with a weak heart. The teacher said he would not be coming back to school. Robert lived in an apartment house not far from school and one day the teacher took us to see him. I can still remember looking up at the window on the third floor and waving and blowing kisses. A few weeks later we heard that Robert was in the hospital and we all sent pictures and letters. We really loved him a lot, and when he died, we were very sad and upset for a long time. (I'm sure today, with all the advances in medicine since I was a child, chances are he could be cured, but this was in the early thirties, when getting sick was much more serious and dangerous.)

Probably the reason I remember Emily and Marian and Robert so well is because these memories show so clearly that kids have so many different emotions and can behave in so many different ways. Sometimes children gang up on one child and can be cruel. Sometimes children gossip about each other, sometimes they tell one person a secret and make other children feel left out. At each stage of growing up, kindness and cruelty, sharing and competing, are natural parts of life. And the main reason for these mixed feelings—and much of the behavior that drives children crazy— is that children feel very insecure, uncertain; they want more than anything else to be popular and successful, and nobody is sure they can succeed. It seems to me that competition is probably never greater than during the grade-school years. I'm sure you and your friends compete with each other about almost everything; clothes, sports, grades, haircuts, holes in jeans, who can spit farthest! Feeling competitive with others is a normal human desire to express oneself, to achieve new skills. That is something we are born with and helps us to grow. A baby wants to learn to crawl, walk, run. There are also many things on the outside that encourage children to feel that they have to compete, try to be better than anyone else. Parents compare one child with another: Joyce's mother says, "I can't understand why you don't do better in math—Diane and Aaron did so well—you're just not working hard enough." I remember that I never understood why it was considered such a terrible crime if one child helped another on a test, when most of the time teachers were telling us to be kind to each other and share.

Sometimes Scout leaders or people in charge of Little League become so ambitious for their own groups that they get carried away with the idea and nothing else matters except winning. Instead of having fun and relaxing, children feel a great deal of anxiety and stress unless they happen to have unusual skills and talents, which everybody cannot have. All of us have our special strengths and weaknesses—we can't excel at everything. But there are great pressures on children to try to be very good at everything.

Competitive feelings also happen when teachers compare children to each other; competitiveness happens when children are separated into groups that make them feel "dumb" or "smart." Instead of making a big fuss about cheating on tests, I believe it would be a good idea if teachers encouraged children to help each other. In schools where this is done, *all* the children do much better.

Outside of school there is a lot of competition too. Often a parent who was not too good at playing baseball really wants a child to be the best. Sometimes parents want their children to have opportunities they never had and insist on piano lessons, ballet lessons, art classes, tennis lessons, boxing lessons, and so on. Any of these activities can be a lot of fun and make a person feel really good, but sometimes these experiences can be spoiled if a child feels he or she *must* try to be best. I used to go to a YMCA pool, and I often saw parents and swim counselors pushing, pushing, pushing—not just to encourage new skills but for a boy or girl to dive or do the breaststroke better than anyone else.

I asked one third grader whether the children in her class had been nicer to each other in first grade or second grade. I was sure she would say second grade. I knew her first-grade teacher had been much more strict and impatient and made some of the children feel they were not as smart as other children. In second grade the teacher was crazy about all the children and encouraged them to be individuals; she never compared them to each other. Because the children were helped to feel really good about themselves, they were kinder to each other. Think back over your years of school and try to remember when the best things happened and when the worst things happened. Very often it will have to do with the messages you got from grownups. The times they made you feel like a failure, the times they made you feel lovable, the times they helped you to know you had many talents, the times they ignored you.

It can be very confusing when parents and teachers tell children to be honest and friendly and helpful to each other. We hear a great deal about people being respected for making a lot of money, for having great power, for being better than anyone else at what they do and pushing other people around in the process. We all know that even some of the people we have come to admire the most, especially athletes, can actually do permanent harm to themselves taking drugs in order to win. Such people hurt themselves in order to achieve success. If adults behave in such ways, how much harder it is for children; if you feel self-conscious and shy and not sure of yourself, too many demands and expectations can be pretty upsetting. In the middle of feeling sad or frightened, if someone makes fun of you for wearing glasses or having braces, or being tall or short, or fat or thin, or having freckles, or being clumsy in gym, it might help you feel better if you would remem-

ber that people who have a need to attack or be-
little another person do so because they think they
can build themselves up, be more important, that
way.

The *why* of kids driving kids crazy has to do
with the feelings we have inside of us and the
things we feel others expect of us. Sometimes the
best way to understand something is by looking
at the opposite side. There is a place we have all
heard about where it is far less common for kids
to drive each other crazy. This is the "Special
Olympics"—for children with a variety of problems and disabilities. Some of the children are
mentally retarded, some of them are paralyzed in
parts of their bodies, some have illnesses like multiple sclerosis and many other conditions which
mean that their lives will be different from those
of most other children.

Have you ever watched one of their Olympics?
How they encourage each other, how they shout
and hug each person when he or she completes an
activity, winning or losing? People with severe
disabilities are never in doubt about being different. It's a fact of life, and the struggle to succeed
to the best of *their own* ability is more important
than to worry about being beautiful or smart or
popular. Of course they wish for such things, but
they know that for them, there are more impor-

tant things to concentrate on. Each child knows that all the other children have equal or worse problems to overcome. They are comrades in a common struggle. The *why* of driving each other crazy is missing. Grownups certainly encourage them to try their best and the young people want to do as well as they can, but the pressure is quite different. No one suggests they should be like someone else; everyone wants each of them to be an individual.

I am sure that what you are most concerned about is the kids who drive *you* crazy. The only way you can change such situations is by understanding them and seeing if it's possible for you to do something about the cause or causes.

Melanie seems to you to be the most stuck-up girl in your class. She hardly ever says a word, never smiles, just does her work and even has lunch by herself. You and your friends wonder who she thinks she is; it drives you a little crazy because you have the feeling she is very critical and thinks none of you are good enough for her.

Rather than being stuck-up, the most likely reason Melanie acts that way is because she is very shy and is afraid none of you will like her. Another possibility is that she's very worried about something that is happening at home. Maybe her mother is very sick or maybe her father lost his job. In my whole life I have never met anyone who was stuck-up because they *really* felt they were better than anyone else. Sometimes even the most popular kid in your class, or the one who gets the best grades or is the captain of the soccer team, probably brags a lot because every young person, successful or not, worries about being popular or staying popular.

What you might do about someone who seems very stuck-up is to sit down next to him or her in the cafeteria or library; you might mention that you are worried about passing history, or, if you are really a brave person you might even admit that you are feeling sad today because nobody invited you to the school dance. Or possibly you might mention that you can't seem to concentrate on what the teacher is saying today, because your parents had a loud argument at breakfast. Of course whatever you say has to be true, but the idea is to let this other kid know you can understand another person's feelings and problems.

There is certainly no guarantee that this person who seems so distant and unfriendly will respond, but it won't drive you as crazy to be ignored if you know you tried.

What I remember drove me crazy when I was in fourth or fifth grade was a girl who was one class ahead of me. She was a friend of my cousin.

My cousin was my age, but she had been skipped—
believe me, *that* drove me crazy because it made
me feel she was smart and I was dumb and I felt
sure it bothered my parents. Jean would be walking to the park playground with her arm around
my cousin and she would tease me unmercifully.
She'd say, "Watch out, there's a big dog coming
after you," when of course there wasn't. She'd make
fun of me if I stumbled or couldn't keep up with
some of the faster walkers. She would mention the
names of boys in my class and shout that I was
in love with one of them. Often she picked the
right one—Stewart—who didn't even know I
existed. She made every trip to the park miserable
for me.

If anyone had asked me at that time why she
did it, I couldn't have figured out any reason. Now,
looking back, I think I know what was going on.
She had figured out that I felt bad about my cousin
being skipped; I was vulnerable to being hurt easily. She made the most of that, thinking my cousin
would then remain her best friend. Many years
later I learned that her father was sent to prison
for "bootlegging." When I was a child there was
a federal law against drinking liquor, but it didn't
really stop anybody. The people who brought liquor into the country and sold it (called bootleg-
gers) were considered criminals, and her father was

caught. I believe it was a very dumb law, but I am sure that at the time Jean must have been terribly worried and ashamed. Making me a target for her painful feelings made her feel better temporarily—somebody else was suffering. But it drove me crazy. If some magic genie could take me back to that time, almost sixty years ago, and if I knew what I know now about people's mixed-up feelings, I'm not sure I could stop Jean's teasing, but I know I would be able to ignore it until she got tired of the game. That's because I know that my feelings of being hurt, of worrying about being popular and smart, were unnecessary because I turned out just fine. The trouble is *you* have no way of knowing what will happen to you—but I can tell you that I am certain that a day will come when you will feel so good about yourself that other kids would have a hard time driving you crazy.

One day a few years ago, I passed the park playground I'd gone to every day in elementary school. By this time I was a grown woman, with a husband and a daughter whom I loved and who loved me. I had written many books. I'd been on television. I was probably the best-known person in my class. Others were of course doing wonderful and exciting things with their lives, but because I had become a writer, my name was even in crossword puzzles sometimes!

Standing, looking at the rocks on which we had played, and remembering being taunted by Jean and always being chosen last for games because I was terrible at team sports, my eyes filled with tears. I thought how wonderful it would have been if I could have had a magic crystal ball and could have seen into the future—to know that even if I was terrible in mathematics and was too chubby and didn't understand grammar, I was going to turn out just fine.

Sometimes, in all probability, you have driven another kid crazy! You may not want to, but you just can't seem to stop yourself. Maybe you make fun of Lester's voice, which is changing, and you imitate the way it squeaks and the other kids laugh. Or maybe you giggle with a couple of other girls in the bathroom when you know Annie is in one of the booths and she's the first girl in the class to begin having menstrual periods, so you laugh and bang on the door and ask her what's going on. I know about Lester and Annie because *I* was once part of such a group and I have felt ashamed about it ever since. *Why* were we so cruel? Now I know it was because the rest of us were confused and scared about the mysteries of growing up; we were nervous and ill at ease about ourselves. We couldn't stop ourselves because we had inner feelings we didn't even know about consciously, and certainly didn't understand. In those days very few grownups talked to us about puberty, the time when changing from a child to an adult begins. No one talked to us about the hormones which bring us into adolescence and change our bodies so dramatically.

Just as we need to ask *why* when someone is unkind to us, we also need to ask *why* when we are driving some other kid crazy. In many ways you are more fortunate than any previous generation, because now feelings are understood better and talked about more. It is now possible for you to try to figure out *why* kids drive kids crazy. And when you really think hard about it you will discover that the reason why is that all children, growing up along with you, worry about being popular and smart and attractive and lovable— and most of us go on feeling this way for many, many years. Quite a few grownups never feel good about themselves and adults can drive each other crazy too, when they don't feel they are worthwhile people. I hope you will realize that the more you come to respect and love yourself as a special and good human being, the less you will drive other kids crazy and the less others will be able to drive you crazy.

One of the main reasons why kids drive other

kids crazy is that they have no way of knowing that a time will come when they will like themselves much more and won't be so easily bothered by the opinions of others.

3

Friends and Enemies: Peer Pressure

The neighbors could hear Melissa yelling at her mother, early one morning. It sounded as if her mother must have been hitting her and for a moment everyone was upset and wondering what they should do. And then they heard what Melissa was screaming: "YOU CAN'T MAKE ME! I'LL KILL MYSELF IF YOU THROW AWAY MY JEANS WITH THE HOLE IN THE KNEE! THEY ARE STILL PERFECT!"

The problem is that Melissa is twelve years old. Hopefully never again in her whole life is she going to worry so much about being exactly like her schoolmates than she will be for the next four or five years. If you are somewhere along the way to adolescence yourself, you probably understand exactly how Melissa felt.

Glen's father had to drag Glen to the barbershop for a haircut. His father and the barber promised to leave a "tail" in the back, but when Glen saw himself in the mirror, he almost burst into tears. He ran out to the car, hid down on the floorboard, and swore he could not go to school for the next six or eight weeks until his hair had grown back; the barber had forgotten about the tail.

Linda, now a grown woman, told me, "I was the youngest of four girls and all my clothes were hand-me-downs. By the time they got to me they were never the right style and I had a miserable childhood because of that one problem." Jonathan's parents were shocked by his sixth-grade report card. Where he had had mostly A's and B's in earlier grades, now he had mostly C's and even one D. They couldn't get a satisfactory explanation from Jonathan, but his teacher told his parents, "Now the most popular kids in the class are the 'jocks,' and Jonathan was embarrassed to be the smartest student in the class. To be popular right now, the kids think it's 'cool' to be interested only in sports."

It's fortunate that peer pressure doesn't last forever! If it did, Melissa would never find the clothes that truly suit her personality and Glen would spend so much of his time worrying about how people cut their hair that he would never have time to study engineering, and Jonathan would never have become a scientist doing research on trying to find a cure for cancer.

Chances are you have heard the expression *peer pressure*. It's the grownups' way of saying what I have already mentioned, that young people feel insecure about themselves. They wonder what they will be like when they grow up; they wonder if they can ever learn long division, or if people will love them—whether or not they will have friends; they wonder if they will be able to go to college and get a good job; they wonder how they will turn out, and they worry quite a lot.

When we worry about ourselves, we want to find some way to feel better. It isn't as comforting as it once was to have your parents approve of you. Now you feel a strong urge to move toward your own generation (your peers) and now it becomes far more important that *they* approve of you. In fact, you probably worry if your parents do approve of you! It seems to mean they are not letting you grow up.

The tall, beautiful girl with blond hair starts wearing a red headband; every girl who wants to be popular gets a red headband. The best soccer player wears his shirt backward, so almost everybody wants shirts they can wear back to front, much to their parents' dismay. The boy who is the smartest in the class comes to school wearing glasses with blue rims. All of a sudden dozens of boys with twenty-twenty vision go home and tell their parents they need glasses—with blue rims!

Peer pressure is wanting to be like others who *appear to be* more sure of themselves. Hopefully when you grow up you will want to be yourself—whether or not that makes you different from others. Right now you want to be exactly like the others you admire most.

Things were easier when the most important people in your life were your family. Even when they got angry, you probably felt they loved you; no matter what family problems there might be, you were pretty sure they would take care of you. Now you are moving, slowly but surely, toward your own generation and it's not easy. Eventually you will realize that there is no way you can possibly be like everyone else, and it would be a great bore if that *were* possible—but for most young people, coming to that conclusion takes many years of growing up.

One of the most common things that happens during elementary school years is something called *scapegoating*. Here is an example of scapegoating:

Three girls live in houses right next to each other. June is ten. She has two older sisters who are smart and pretty and make her feel she's dumb and ugly. The two neighbors, Arlene and Terry, are both seven years old and in the same class. They usually have a terrific time playing imaginary games or Monopoly and Parcheesi with each other. June hasn't made any close friends and isn't doing well in school. She's lonely and unhappy when she comes home. Over and over again she interrupts whatever Arlene and Terry are doing; she plays one against the other; she says she wants to be friends with Terry but not with Arlene because "she's really a jerk and a nerd." Terry feels honored to have been chosen by an older and more sophisticated girl—June wears high heels, lipstick, and long earrings to school, and Terry thinks she's really something. Arlene is deeply hurt and runs off crying. She and Terry have lost each other for a few days. The following week June lets them know she thinks Arlene is much better than Terry at "Simon Says." June makes it seem like a matter of life or death who wins. When Terry loses, June laughs and Arlene is so caught up in this new approval by June that she laughs too. Terry is very hurt and runs home.

Sometimes parents have to step in when children get caught in this kind of trap of playing one child against another, which ends up in some-one feeling insecure and hurt. Terry's and Arlene's mothers suggested that maybe both girls really had a crush on June—she was older and appeared to be so strong and confident that they wanted her approval at any price. They told Terry and Arlene that June was really unhappy and lonely and needed them more than they needed her. One day, when Arlene and Terry were playing in Terry's house and June came over, Arlene said, "Listen, June, you can play with us, but not if you can't play with *both* of us. It's either all together or you can't stay." June was being accepted, but with condi-tions which she knew were really quite fair.

Not all problems are solved easily, because every child feels insecure and wants to be popular. Yes, I said *every child.* The show-offs, the most boast-ful, the smartest, and the best-looking kids worry just like all the others about being admired.

When I was in grade school, I thought I would just die because Phyllis was the most beautiful and smartest girl in the class, and the boy I had a crush on, Stewart, was crazy about her. It was very hard for me to think about what I was sup-posed to be studying. I both hated and envied Phyllis. Another girl, Jane, was very rich and pretty. She was terrific in math and always seemed so sure of herself—I would have been thrilled if I

could have changed places with her. Carl and
Walter were handsome, and they seemed to me to
be smarter and more popular than I could ever be.
They seemed so self-confident and never paid any
attention to me at all.

Once in awhile I would be asked to join some
club. There was a "Tarzan Club," but I always
got some minor part like Cheetah's cousin. There
was a book we girls all loved and cried over, *Little
Women* by Louisa May Alcott, and I was asked to
join a "Little Women's Club," not as one of the
interesting daughters but as the mother. I was always getting the mother part in school plays. In
Alice in Wonderland I played the big, ugly Duch-
ess. I was always jealous of other children and always felt I would never be as successful as anyone
else. That was "peer pressure" coming from inside
me.

Mitsuko and Bernice became best friends at the
beginning of fourth grade. They had sleep-overs,
they played together every day at recess, they sat
together on the school bus, called each other on
the telephone, and Mitsuko's parents often took
Bernice on weekend trips with the family. They
told each other their deepest secrets and swore
eternal love. In March Bernice began to realize
that Mitsuko was avoiding her. She was spending

more and more time with a girl in the fifth grade. Finally, the last time they spent an afternoon together, Mitsuko yelled at her in the middle of a game, "This is too babyish for me, I'm not interested in playing games anymore!"

Bernice was devastated—she cried when she went to bed at night, she couldn't concentrate on her homework, she told her mother she wasn't hungry. She said she felt sick and couldn't go to school and felt as if she would die when her parents made her go. She sat as far away from Mitsuko and her new friend on the bus as she could. About one week later a girl named Selma sat down next to her. Selma was shy and nobody at school had taken much notice of her. There didn't seem to be anything special about her. She whispered to Bernice, "I know how awful you feel. The same thing happened to me in my Brownie troop last year." For most of the rest of the school year, Bernice and Selma were best friends. In the summertime Bernice went to camp, and Selma went to see her father who lived so far away she never got to see him except during the summer. When the fall came each girl had made other friends and had very little to do with each other ever again. Although this friendship didn't last, it did provide a Band-Aid for hurt feelings and helped both girls to become more compassionate.

I'm sure all of you have had such experiences and probably felt that you had failed, that you'd never get over it, and that something terrible had happened. Not true; such experiences are not only normal, they are also absolutely necessary. You are learning and growing and changing, and you need to experiment, to experience many different relationships before you know what you are really looking for, what will satisfy your needs, and what you can give to other people. Did you ever hear of a Swedish smorgasbord? It is a table loaded with many different kinds of food—like a buffet—and the idea is to taste everything and see which things you like. While you are growing up you need a smorgasbord of friends for the same reason.

Larry and José were best friends for a long time. Both of them were interested in dinosaurs and spent a lot of Saturdays at the museum. They both loved baseball and basketball. But Larry wasn't much interested in school and was just barely getting by. He said he wanted to be an auto mechanic in his father's garage when he got out of high school. José loved school, spent extra time in the library, was determined to go to college and become a lawyer. They lost touch with each other as they grew and changed. They needed new and different kinds of friends. Larry played baseball after school almost every day and his friends were his teammates. José and Ben had a special project for their seventh-grade class, having to do with environmental pollution in their city. They spent time visiting many city agencies and interviewing people. Their project was so good that they won a school award for it.

Some friendships that seem very important at the moment have to do with something special that we need from another person. My teachers became so worried about my friendship with Claire that they called my parents to school. We were in the seventh grade. I was overweight and felt very unattractive. No boys paid any attention to me. At school dances I was always a wallflower. I tried hard not to go to them, but sometimes I had to. Claire was very sophisticated. She wore the most expensive and fashionable clothes. She wore net stockings, high heels, and makeup, and when I was young, such things were supposed to be signs of being "loose." At that time it meant that she probably let a lot of boys kiss her! I thought she was wonderful. I loved to go shopping with her. She had to show every dress to her father, who spent a great deal of time on how she looked. My father seemed more interested in my mind—he never noticed what I was wearing. I was envious of the time and attention Claire's father gave to her appearance.

My parents were smarter than the teachers; they said they weren't worried—that I would get over Claire when I was ready. The next year, having gained some useful ideas from Claire about my appearance and ways of talking to boys, I was more self-confident. Now my best friend was Madeline. Her older brother belonged to an astronomy club, and while neither of us had much interest in the stars, there were about twenty boys and only three girls in the club. I spent most of my adolescence with this group. We were all struggling to become "intellectuals," to talk about politics and philosophy and religion. We began going to the theater and ballet together. I was getting a little closer to becoming the person I would be as an adult. These were just the kinds of friends I needed. (I even married one of them!)

Young people have more physical energy than most adults. Having to sit still for long hours in school means that when school is over, there may be some pretty rough play, sometimes ending in fights. What often happens is that before long there are opposing gangs; instead of individual fights, several children join together to fight another group. One of the reasons this happens is that the "enemy" is not really very important; what is important is that each individual feels guaranteed the friendship in his or her own group.

The kind of friendships that occur where a group feels there is a common enemy may be very intense and may even become dangerous, and we need to think carefully about what they mean and what is happening. Marty, who is smaller than some of the others in his class, joined a gang—they wanted him because he always had money to buy sodas after school. Sometimes they found ways to get cigarettes illegally, and even though Marty never wanted to become a smoker, he went along with the group so they would respect him. One day on the way home from school, the group noticed a new house that was just being built. Brian thought it would be a great game to throw rocks at the new windows, and Dick and Paul agreed. For Marty this was going too far—he felt this was wrong, and he left the gang and went home. He was shaking when he got home and his mother asked what was wrong. When he told her, she said, "That was a very brave thing to do. You are not the kind of person those boys want you to be, and I'm glad you found out now before they do something even worse or more serious." Marty was scared to go to school—he didn't know what would happen. The others teased him and made fun of him at lunch in the cafeteria and called him a sissy and a coward, and then they ignored him; they too had realized that he was really not one of them.

A most important fact is that a young person is most unlikely to do something he or she knows is wrong, all alone. Something new occurs when boys and girls are in a group. There can be a feeling of excitement and a strong bond of comradeship. It is an adventurous feeling, a feeling of belonging to something bigger than oneself.

I made a list of things that any kid would know are wrong. The list included taking money from an old lady, breaking into a house and stealing a TV set, taking a new football away from a younger child, writing dirty words on the wall of a church, teasing some younger children by taking their coats and waving them around over their heads in winter. Some of the things I mentioned were not very serious; others were quite serious. Almost every kid I asked said these were things they would never do all by themselves but only if they felt they had to go along with the gang, or lose their place in the group.

Because groups will often do things individuals would not do, there are certain places that seem to stimulate poor behavior. For example, school buses are often the place where kids get wild, fight, call each other mean names, or get very overexcited. The playground, parks, and streets, when no grownups are around, may become at certain times places you want to avoid when you notice that other children are beginning to behave in ways you don't like or which make you feel afraid.

There are times when you have to ask yourselves whether or not a particular friendship or group of friends might be harmful. It's very hard to figure out why you need a certain individual or gang. If anyone had asked me why I liked Claire, I probably could not have explained it, but since we weren't doing anything that could hurt other people, it was not a harmful relationship. If you get into a situation where you discover that your three closest friends are buying marijuana after school, and you know that it is something that can only harm you, you have to ask yourself why they have become your best friends. Do they seem tough and you feel like a weakling? Are you angry at your parents and want to defy them? Is it that you feel others are impressed that they included you? Sometimes we have to have the strength to say, "This is not for me." It's not easy, but it may be very important. It is great to try a lot of different kinds of friendships, but some may be hazardous to your health!

Learning to say "no" in some situations may often be one of the first ways in which we discover who we really are, and that we can have courage and wisdom in making our own decisions. Because of the terrible epidemic of drugs it has never been more important to have the courage to say "no" than it is today.

Peer pressure helps young people feel safe while they go through the often frightening process of growing up. In many ways, trying to be exactly like your friends for awhile is comforting. It helps to give you the encouragement you need to begin moving away from the greater safety of being a little child taken care of by your parents. But there are some times when peer pressure can become dangerous, not only when it might encourage you to do something with a group that you wouldn't do alone, but when you know right away, whether in a group or not, it will be important to protect yourself, even if it interferes with being popular.

Lee was invited to a party by one of the boys in his class. He was surprised and very happy. He had come as a Cambodian refugee to this country just six months before, and this was the first party he had been invited to. He had been raised very strictly by his parents, and when he got to the party he realized at once that Richard's parents were not at home, that beer was being served and some of the kids in his class were already drunk, and that some girls and boys had gone into the bedrooms and locked the doors. He had never seen anything like this, and he was scared. Pretty soon the other people at the party realized how shocked

Lee was and they began taunting him, making fun of his accent, slanting their eyes, dancing around him. Lee began to cry and that just made everyone laugh harder. Lee ran out the door and down the street. He soon realized he wasn't sure which way to go to get home. Eventually a police car went by, saw him sitting on the curb looking miserable, and took him home. For the rest of the school year he avoided everyone. He decided American children and their families were terrible. He did his work and went right home. His school was overcrowded, and none of the teachers noticed how isolated Lee was. Most of the other new students came from Spanish-speaking countries and they all banded together.

Lee was never able to tell his parents about the party. He just said he was tired and decided to leave early. Sometime later his older sister heard about the party and she told him, "Not all American families are like those where the parents are not home. I made friends with a girl named Nancy who told me that whenever you are invited to a party where there are going to be lots of people, you should always arrange to know where your parents can be reached by phone to come and get you if you want to leave. She said most parents stay home to supervise parties."

But what if you know everybody very well and

they are your friends? You never dreamed the party would be unsupervised and get so wild. Would you have the courage to call your family and leave? At the moment of decision you may have the feeling that you are making a mistake if you call, that you will never have a friend afterward. Not true; in the first place it is more than likely that a few others are as uncomfortable as you are and will, at least secretly, admire your courage. Secondly, in the years to come you will feel more and more proud of yourself for having a mind of your own. You know that alcohol and drugs and too much "fooling around" is not appropriate at this time in your life. The truth is that deep down you really would prefer to have adults set some regulations and rules. The problem is that you feel embarrassed and worried about being called a "mama's baby," but one way around this is to tell your friends your parents are driving you crazy but there is nothing you can do about it. They don't need to know that *you* asked your mother to find out if any grownups would be supervising a party you have been invited to!

During the years when peer pressure is so strong, it may help to make your parents or other adults the villains. It's not that *you* don't think it's a great idea to go for a ride with the seventeen-year-old older brother of your best friend, who just got his license, and you may scream and yell at your parents for saying "not on your life," but secretly, if you are at all a sensible person, you know such an adventure might be dangerous. It is a good idea to think about possible consequences of the things you want to do or are encouraged by others to do.

Peer pressure makes your relationships with parents and teachers more difficult at times. Being "teacher's pet" can be a heavy burden, since the kids in your class won't like that a bit. Or, on the other hand, being ridiculed by a teacher when you are at the blackboard and can't figure out a math problem is just as bad, because you worry more about losing the respect of your classmates than finding the answer to the question.

Young people who want to be as much like everyone else as possible have a very hard time with parents who are genuine individuals and have long since stopped worrying about having to please other people all the time. My husband and I like to wear comfortable clothes. My husband almost never wears a tie, and when our daughter was in elementary school, he drove a funny-looking, rickety foreign car. I never wore high heels or worried about being stylish, and I used almost no makeup. When our daughter, Wendy, was twelve years old and found out that her parents were to chaperon a school dance, she said she wasn't going to go—she was too ashamed of us. Not only do kids worry about how *they* look to their friends, they worry about how their *parents* look as well. We finally compromised. My husband and I agreed to stay at the far end of the room behind some large plants and decorations! When her father drove her to school in his crazy old car, wearing a fisherman's hat, Wendy would hide on the floor of the car so no one could see her. Wendy is a grown woman now, and I think what she likes best about her dad and me is that we are different from anybody else she knows. While right now it is normal for you to feel embarrassed by your parents, that is a temporary state of affairs.

It is normal to feel angry and rebellious and to side with your own age group against your parents on every issue. But there is another kind of feeling, equally normal and necessary, and that is the wish that your mother and father will help you to be safe and not make really big mistakes. Peer pressure often encourages breaking rules: watching too much TV instead of doing homework, drinking some wine or liquor at a friend's house and getting a little sick, making too much noise and upsetting people in buses and on the street, showing off by jumping from the top of a garage—all things you would not do if you weren't worried about being popular. The truth today (and this is possibly the best-kept secret among your friends) is that a lot of young people wish that adults would pay more attention to them and make and enforce good rules.

Many years ago I was having a discussion with a group of parents who were talking about discipline. One woman said, "When I was young my parents owned a small grocery store. They worked there about eighteen hours a day. My sisters and brothers and I had to take care of ourselves a lot of the time. I'd hear other mothers yelling out the window to their kids, 'Come back, you didn't finish your breakfast,' or, 'It's going to snow—come here and put on your boots.' Their children would yell and carry on, and I was *jealous*. I wished my parents would pay more attention to me." All young people have mixed feelings. On the one hand you want to grow up and become part of your own generation, and on the other hand you know you and your friends are not really ready to be independent, make all your own decisions, give in to every impulse.

While you are trying so hard to be just like your friends it might not be a bad idea for you to look around; who are the grownups you admire the most? Whether relatives or famous people or teachers or neighbors, my guess is the people you like and respect the most are the people with strong minds of their own—interesting *individuals*. Hopefully that will become your goal as you learn that the best kinds of friends are the people who want you to be *yourself*.

4

Boys and Girls

It's all very exciting and confusing. You are beginning to have feelings that are new and different. Perri may seem noisy and sloppy and forever
showing off, but she wants boys to like her, and
she pays a lot of attention to them. Boys make
her feel funny inside. Sometimes she wants some
special boy to notice her and want to be with her,
even if his friends tease him. Howard is very confused about girls. One minute they act as if they
hate boys, the next minute they giggle together
and Howard knows they are flirting with him; the
next minute a girl he likes a lot turns out to be a
better pitcher than he is and that makes him feel
bad, and then another day she's all dressed up and

she keeps telling him how she thinks he will end up on a major-league baseball team. *Why* does she say that when Howard knows she's a better athlete? Why does she want to flatter him? Why does there seem to be more tension now between boys and girls? Both sexes are excited, confused, and seem to behave differently with each other every day.

Millie doesn't understand why one day Carlos wants to carry her books for her after school, and on another day he ignores her completely and is too busy talking to his gang of friends to even notice her. Joe is secretly crazy about a girl in his class, and one day she brings him cookies she made herself. The next day he sees her laughing with her girlfriends, and he has the feeling they are laughing at him. Kenneth likes to look at Nina and he even dreams about her, but in school he hates her because she's smarter than he is. What's this all about? It's about growing up, beginning to learn how it feels to be a man or a woman, and sometimes that's exciting and fun, and sometimes it's annoying and upsetting.

When your great-grandparents were growing up, boys and girls were separated in some of the strangest ways. Very often, for example, there were separate entrances to schools—boys in one door, girls in another. Once inside, they might be allowed to learn in the same classrooms, but they never played together, because boys were supposed to be strong and rough and girls were supposed to be sweet, gentle, and weak. Gym classes and all sports were separate. Boys teased girls, and girls flirted and gossiped about boys. Boys felt they had to be superior to girls in every way, which was quite a burden. Girls felt they had to be submissive and subservient, which was quite unfair.

It is harder now to figure out what it means to be a boy or a girl than it ever was in all human history. Knights in armor knew exactly what to do—go out and fight. Nice little girls during the time of Queen Victoria wore clothing that made it hard for them to move. Their corsets were so tight that they often fainted in hot weather, but that was fine because ladies were supposed to faint. Even when both men and women worked equally hard to survive on their farms or eventually in factories, mothers were supposed to raise the children and fathers were supposed to make all the decisions.

Today there is another foolish idea, and that is that boys and girls are *exactly* alike. The good idea that every person should have equal rights is often misinterpreted to mean that any person, of either sex, is the same as any other person.

I'm not sure who had a tougher time growing

up—the generations that tried to separate boys and girls, or your generation, in which there is so much confusion about what it means to be a boy or a girl, a man or a woman. Rather than having limited contact with each other, you are likely to be together in cooking classes and on the baseball field. It is far more difficult today for boys and girls to figure out how to get along with each other. The reason is that there are now so many more choices, so many more kinds of behavior and activities that are shared.

It might be interesting to ask your grandparents what it was like when they were growing up. They will probably tell you that very few girls grew up to be doctors or lawyers or physicists. In many families boys were sent to college, but not their sisters, no matter how smart they were. It was expected that girls would get married and raise children and men would support their families. Some things were right and proper for boys to do, and some were right for girls to do, and very few rebels tried to change the rules.

For example, looking back it seems strange to me that when I went to college there were very strict rules about what time we girls had to be back in the dormitory at night, while the boys had no such rules at all. Now it seems strange to me that I was almost the only one of my girlfriends to get a master's degree and have a profession. The majority of my friends stayed home all the time with their children. Men and women seemed to accept the rules. And girls who were very smart in subjects like mathematics or engineering often tried to hide such facts because they thought boys wouldn't like them. And boys sometimes suffered through sports they didn't enjoy because they thought girls wouldn't think they were masculine enough if they didn't.

I imagine there may be moments when you wish there still were simple rules, when each sex accepted very different (and in many ways unequal) roles. But difficult as it may be for you to figure out what it means to be a man or a woman now, you are luckier. All people now have more choices and are much freer to use their talents and develop their own interests.

In some ways boys and girls haven't changed at all. They can be shy with each other; they can be attracted to each other and not know what to do about it. They can pine after someone they feel is unattainable. They can tease a lot to cover feeling embarrassed and uneasy as they realize they are growing up, that the boys' voices may be beginning to change or that the girls' figures are beginning to "fill out." Both sexes are excited as well as fearful about all the changes that are going to

take place in the next few years. The most admired in their classes are still girls who are pretty
and boys who are good athletes. Girls giggle and
talk about boys; boys frequently tell wild (and un-
true!) stories about getting girls to kiss them, even
"make out." Boys and girls want to be liked by
the opposite sex and will try hard to attract attention. At the very same time they will sometimes
feel they would rather just be with their own sex.
For example, boys may feel that it seems like too
much of an effort to try to understand girls. For
this reason, for a time they may want to join clubs
for boys only, and girls may want only to be around
other girls. These same feelings happened to your
grandparents and your parents too because some
things don't really change.

What is different for you is that ideas about
men and women have changed and now it is very
hard to see differences in the sexes by what they
do. The differences today are mostly in feelings
and may be very hard to define. If you see someone wrestling and another person wearing an apron
it used to be possible to figure out very quickly
who was the man and who was the woman. Now
the man may be wearing the apron and the woman
might be the wrestler.

Until very recently, men were supposed to be
strong and run things; women were supposed to

be weaker and to need taking care of. It was all right for men to be interested in sex; women were supposed to be innocent and helpless. Men were considered smarter than women. Women were supposed to stay home and cook and clean, wash and sew, while men chopped wood, plowed the fields, disciplined the children. Men earned the money and gave some of it to their wives for food and clothing. Boys worked with their fathers, girls learned how to be homemakers from their mothers.

It may sound simple, but the problem was that none of these ideas, rules, and regulations were accurate or made any sense at all. Now you know that there is a girl in your class who is a mathematical genius and a boy who loves to take care of his baby sister. Liz wins all the races; George wants to design clothes when he grows up. The kids in school are all afraid of Beverly—she can beat up anyone. Jacob wins prizes at the county fair for his homemade jelly. What's going on? What is going on is that we have learned that while boys and girls are surely different in many important ways, they have more in common than anyone once believed. While it may be much more difficult to be sure just what it means to be male or female, human beings are finally being permitted to be themselves.

Boys are being told that there is no reason they and their fathers shouldn't wash dishes, take care of babies, cook dinner. At the same time they have the feeling they want to show off, they want to be bigger and stronger, they want to be better at baseball and learning about computers. If girls can do everything boys can do, how are you supposed to feel about being masculine?

Girls are being encouraged to become fire fighters and astronauts, to become athletes and architects. At the same time it often feels good to have a mother who stays with you when you feel sick, and you feel that mothers and fathers hug and kiss their children in different ways. Maybe your mother hopes you will grow up to be a famous surgeon and your father calls you his "little princess" and loves you to wear party dresses and hair ribbons. This is all very confusing.

Once, when I was a nursery-school teacher, Suzy was playing in the doll corner when her mother came to visit the school. Mrs. Karter was terribly upset. "Why is my child in the doll corner?" she asked, as if that was something terrible. Suzy loved playing mommy to the baby doll, but her mother wanted her to be playing with trucks and blocks and puzzles. "I definitely don't want Suzy to get the idea that she can just be a mother," she told us. Sometimes it seems that grownups have just changed sides and still don't really believe in choices.

Seymour may wonder if it's okay to have a fight with a girl, or whether you have to protect girls from getting hurt—but when he grows up, he can be a husband and a father and a nurse. Krissy knows she can decide whether or not she wants to be a wife and a mother, or cross the ocean in a small sailing boat, or race cars, or become a major in the army. Young people today can develop their own dreams, whatever they may be. That's the good part. The hard part is that so much freedom to decide what you want to be, what you want to do, can be confusing and it often feels more like a heavy burden than a privilege.

You get so many different messages from adults. Claudio's father thinks his teacher must be a wimp; why else would a man be teaching first grade? Claudio's mother stays home, cooks, and cleans, and never talks back to his father, who bellows loudly if anyone doesn't do what he says. Max's parents each have part-time jobs; both of them do housework and take care of Max and his two brothers. His father is an editor on the night shift of a newspaper, and his mother works during the day in a library. They seem to be equal partners in every way. Roberta hears her mother complaining all the time about having to work so hard all day as a secretary and then come home and do all the shopping and cooking and cleaning. Roberta's mother and father fight a lot because her father thinks he's doing quite enough if he does the laundry once in awhile. *His* mother never went out to work. Roberta's mother says, "Of course not. Your father earned enough money to support his family!"

The truth is that your parents, and all the grownups you know, are having an equally hard time learning new ways of thinking about their relationships to each other as men and women.

You are growing up in the middle of a revolution! I suppose one might say this revolution started when women began demanding the right to vote. And the revolution got a special push in the 1960's, when a woman by the name of Betty Friedan wrote a book called *The Feminine Mystique.* She felt that after World War Two, when many families moved to the suburbs to raise their children, women often felt like prisoners in their homes, unable to fulfill their own ambitions and talents.

Some mothers and fathers are very excited and enthusiastic about the "Women's Movement" that followed. They enjoy being equal partners and having the opportunity to experience many different roles. Some parents may be shocked by so much change, so fast. They may have grown up in very traditional homes, and some mothers still believe that they should be at home when you return from school, and don't want careers. Some husbands get very upset when a wife wants to start going to college in the hope of becoming a psychologist or a teacher. Some men would get upset if their wife took a course in auto mechanics and learned how to fix a car much better than they could. Some men and women shrink at the idea of a woman trying to save them in a fire, or of a policewoman with a gun in her holster.

Living in changing times is both a blessing and a curse. On the one hand, you will have to make many more tough decisions for yourself and will have a hard time deciding how you feel about being male or female. But you can, if you figure it out for yourself. You will become distinctly your own person, a unique individual, doing things you love to do, having much greater freedom to become the person you want to be.

There is a girl in Philip's sixth-grade math class that drives him crazy. Tess is very pretty, and sometimes Philip has dreams about her. She has long red hair and green eyes, and he can't take his eyes off her when she walks down the hall in a kind of slinky way. She laughs a lot and teases Philip because he hates team sports and is a book-worm. Philip wishes he had the courage to talk to Tess but he's too shy—and she's very popular. In addition to being attracted to Tess, he also hates her! She is the best math student in the class, and he is one of the worst. It makes him feel like a nerd when she goes to the blackboard and works out a very difficult problem and he has no idea what she is doing. Philip is finding out that love and hate sometimes go hand in hand!

Philip's father is a lawyer. He hates team sports too. He'd much rather sit and read a book or listen to music in the evening. Philip has sometimes wished his father would want to teach him baseball—how to hit, how to catch—but his father prefers to talk about the evening news. His mother seems to be very happy staying at home and being a housewife. She spends most of her time with his two sisters, who are more interested in makeup and clothes than anything else. His sisters are a good deal older than Philip, and all they talk about is boys and dates and getting married when they finish high school. None of the women in Philip's family in any way resemble Tess; she is a puzzle to him. She talks about going to Harvard or M.I.T. and becoming a physicist. She treats boys the same way she treats girls, as pals.

Tess's parents are the opposite of Philip's. Her father was a jock all through school. He coaches a famous basketball team. He is always doing something—running, riding a bike, going to a gym. The only time he seems to sit still is when he's watching a sports event on television. Tess's mother is the head of a hospital laboratory and is doing special research on a cure for cancer. Tess is their only child and she's learned to take care of herself after school. She admires both of her parents and knows that when she grows up, she too will do something really interesting. She enjoys reading, studying, going to science museums, and she's earning money for college by baby-sitting and clearing snow from neighors' driveways during the winter.

Philip and Tess have been growing up with very different ideas about what it means to be male and female. Philip expected girls to be very different from boys. Tess expects she can do anything she wants to do.

Victor wishes there hadn't been a Women's Liberation Movement. He would love it if his mother didn't go to work every day but stayed home and served him milk and homemade cookies when he got home from school. Penny wishes her parents didn't push her so hard about her schoolwork—she just wants to get married and have a big family when she grows up. Jawal wishes that girls were more like the ones he knew at home before his father came to work at the United Nations. They were shy and quiet and they never hit boys or tried to be smarter. Maybe these distinctions made life easier, but now we know that different people need different things and we get into trouble unless each person grows up free to choose the kind of activities that he or she will need to feel good about his or her life.

Victor doesn't realize that even if he gets store-bought cookies, his mother is a much happier (and therefore nicer) person to live with because she enjoys what she is doing. And Penny doesn't realize she might change her mind about what she wants to do. Perhaps in high school she will discover that she is fascinated by botany, get excellent marks in class, and begin to feel that she wants very much to study ecology and help to save endangered plants and animals. Maybe she won't change at all, but it is much better to have more choices. If Jawal stays in the United States for a long time, he may begin to enjoy the fact that there are no longer strict rules about what men or women may do and that this makes life more interesting.

Friendships between boys and girls have always been a little complicated. Most boys and girls tend to be more shy with the opposite sex. There is also a special kind of excitement in girl–boy friendships. Boys still enjoy showing off, teasing, flirting. Some girls still like to act helpless—they love it if a boy offers to put his jacket around their shoulders if they feel cold. Both boys and girls get jealous if someone they have a special feeling for is more interested in someone else. Boys worry about being called "sissies." A girl may become angry or embarrassed if someone calls her a "tomboy" just because she wears jeans and old shirts of her father's and can climb a tree as easily as a cat. Girls still get jealous of boys who they feel may have more privileges. Boys feel anxious and threatened if girls seem to be as strong, smart, and athletic as they are. Boys are sometimes annoyed when girls become very aggressive and call them up on the phone constantly.

These things still happen because, despite all the changes and greater equality, boys and girls remain different. Biologically and psychologically they feel and react in ways that are different from each other, and they mature at different rates of growth—girls usually earlier. What a terribly dull world it would be if both sexes were exactly alike. Sex differences *do* matter. Girls can grow up to be mothers; they will develop breasts. Boys can't really imagine what that feels like. Girls don't have ejaculations ("wet dreams") when they reach puberty. They can't imagine how that feels. Girls will begin to menstruate when they reach puberty; no

boy can fully imagine what that must be like.
Inside each male and female are different feelings,
different hormones, different patterns of growth,
different sizes of bones and organs.

I hope that when you were much younger you
enjoyed Fred Rogers of *Mr. Rogers' Neighborhood* as
much as I still do. He wrote a song about boys
and girls which said, "Boys are fancy on the outside, girls are fancy on the inside." This fact of
nature means that there are some kinds of feelings, fantasies, and attitudes that will go on being
different all through your lives no matter what
boys and girls, men and women, may actually do.

During the first years of the Women's Movement there was high excitement about equality of
the sexes. One woman even wrote a book about a
little boy who was given the name "X," so that
he wouldn't feel he was different from girls. I
thought that was a terrible book. I hope you will
grow up feeling that it's just fine to be one sex or
the other; that even while we need to respect each
other and have equal opportunities, each person
will know what he or she feels about being a male
or female, and will enjoy being one or the other
in special and different ways.

Your special feelings will come from inside you,
not from what anyone tells you on the outside.
What people *do* is no longer an easy way to tell

what they *are*. But if you have seen your father cooking spaghetti, or ironing his shirts, you still know he is a man and there is no doubt about it when he puts his arm around your mother. And if your mother manages a bank, you still know she's a woman when she rumples your father's hair and teases him, and you surely know they feel special differences in each other which they enjoy very much when they go away for a weekend by themselves.

Now that some of the television programs that were on twenty to thirty years ago are being brought back, you can see a great difference in attitudes about what it means to be feminine and masculine. The earlier situation comedies, like *Leave It to Beaver* and *Father Knows Best* all showed husbands going out to work and wives staying home. In a program like *The Cosby Show,* you now see a doctor and a lawyer raising a family, but you also see that, whatever they may be doing, they are just crazy about each other. They sure do know which one is the man and which one the woman!

There are ways for boys and girls to become good friends, to learn a lot about each other, to learn to talk to each other. The best ways are not formal dances and parties, or single dating too soon. Going out with a group—skating, picnicking, going to a movie—gives boys and girls a chance to learn about each other without feeling self-conscious or shy. When Carla found out that Edward was interested in saving the dolphins and the whales, she invited him to go along to a meeting of Greenpeace. Having a date with one person is easier, at first, if you choose to do something or have a project about which you can talk to each other easily. Going to baseball or hockey games together, if both young people are interested in sports, is an easier way to get to know each other than going to a school dance where everyone is worrying about being popular. The more shy and tongue-tied a person feels, the more it helps to find common interests. Carol was very nervous the first time she was supposed to ask a boy to go to a friend's party. Suppose the boy she chose said no? All through life boys and girls, men and women, need to realize that if we never take risks, we will never do anything! Failure is not so terrible. We learn a great deal from the things that go wrong. If Carol finds that the first person she asks isn't interested, she needs to think of someone who might be very flattered to be asked. She might find out that although Bob is not the most popular boy in the class, he is kind and thoughtful and when he talks about his great interest in marine biology, she learns some fascinating things. We all become much less self-conscious when we ask another person to tell us about him- or her-self. The truth is that very often the most shy person is thinking too much about him- or herself. Being interested in others and caring about *their* feelings can relieve extreme feelings of shyness.

Learning to be friends helps us begin to decide what kind of people we want to be when we grow up; what kind of people make us feel good, what kind of people upset us, make us angry. We are learning about caring for someone else, and you are learning that all boys and all girls have dreams inside of them about what they want to do when they are grown up.

For your generation there is a new fact that is both confusing and exciting and that is that what-ever your sex, there are few limits on what you can choose to do, depending on your interests and talents.

I promise that as you grow and change, you will learn how you feel about being a man or a woman. What is most important is that however we feel and whatever we do, we are glad to be ourselves and we are interested and respectful and admiring of each other person.

5

Growing Up Faster

Even if you knew exactly how you felt and how to behave, there would be another complication in being boys and girls together.

One very big difference between your growing-up years and that of your parents or grandparents is that you are growing up much faster. I was still playing with dolls when I was eleven or twelve. Boys and girls didn't go out on dates until they were about fifteen. It was considered pretty daring to play "Spin the Bottle" at parties when we were twelve or thirteen. When the friend I mentioned earlier, Claire, wore high heels in junior high school, she was considered "cheap." I pleaded with my mother to let me use an almost colorless lipstick when I was fourteen. I never saw a movie until I was eight, I never ate in a foreign restaurant until I was about twelve. I never saw any pornographic magazines, or passed by theaters showing pictures of nude people having sex.

Young people are growing up much faster these days. They have better nutrition and fewer serious illnesses—such as diphtheria, smallpox, or polio—and they appear to be growing up more quickly and reaching puberty earlier. In addition, they are living in a society that is constantly tempting and exciting them with earlier exposure to sexual ideas and fantasies.

What this does to friendships is that both boys and girls become more self-conscious with each other, feel that they are expected to act as if they were adults. It is a well-kept secret that even the most sophisticated of your classmates who may talk about dates and "making out" are probably lying a lot, or are scared, no matter what they are doing, and are not mature enough to know as much as they need to know about the feelings and responsibilities that are a part of becoming an adult.

Your parents have a problem that is much more difficult than ever before, and that is being able to control what you may see and hear. For example, there are now telephone numbers you can call for pornographic sex talk. The only control a parent can have is to lock the telephone or do his or her best to get your cooperation in understanding that the kind of messages you can get on 900 numbers, having to do with sexual talk and fantasies, are going to upset you. The telephone messages are overstimulating—many young people have had upsetting dreams for a long time after listening to them. Most of all, telephone exchanges or pornographic magazines or movies or television programs, give you a very distorted idea about sex. They make you feel that sex is a mechanical matter—all one has to do is learn *techniques,* almost like directions for building a car motor. You and your parents have probably muttered angrily over the directions for putting a toy or a piece of furniture together, such as, "A fits into B and is crossed over to C while D and E have two bolts (F and G) that must be screwed into H."

Mechanical objects, machinery, are not at all like human beings who have feelings. Too much exposure to mechanical sexual stimulation at too early an age can become a source of worry and anxiety. This material can easily make a young person think that he or she will fail miserably at what appears to be a most demanding task. When you are older, you will begin to have feelings which will help you to understand that techniques are very far from the most important part of sexual relationships. What can never be explained by pornography is *caring about another person.* When young men and woman begin to fall in love, the most important part of that feeling is being together, learning together, and taking care of each other.

I feel quite uncomfortable when I see young people in elementary school and junior high school looking at the pictures outside a porno movie theater or watching very explicit scenes of lovemaking in movies and on television. The reason I'm shocked is that when I was young we were protected from such experiences. In fact, few of our parents knew as many facts about sex as you probably do by sixth or seventh grade! By the time I was twelve I knew where babies came from and not much more!

I don't think that was such a bad thing. When I was thirteen I belonged to a young people's club. One night a doctor came and discussed sex with the girls in the group. I went home and told my parents, "I think it's all disgusting! I'm *never* going to do *that!*" My parents smiled and my mother said, "Never try to anticipate emotion." Many years later I understood exactly what she meant. There are many experiences for which a person has to be ready in mind and body before he or she can fully understand the meaning of the experience. Once a person becomes mature, both in physical and emotional ways, it is easy to understand that sex is not at all ugly and unnatural. Once a person is mature enough to understand about falling in love and being responsible for another person, and really caring what happens to her or him, then it is possible to stop acting silly and excited, and sometimes reckless.

The problem for you, in today's world, is that you are likely to "know" everything—all the facts —but nature is going about its own business as it always has, and you are not yet mature enough to know what to think or feel or do with all these facts. We know, for example, that boys and girls who start heavy necking, petting, even having sexual intercourse, at a very early age almost always have bad experiences. There is disappointment, fear of disease and pregnancy, and a heavy burden of secrecy.

Janet has five brothers and sisters. Her father died when she was only two years old and her mother has had to support the family by working long hours. Janet is the oldest child and she has carried a heavy load of shopping, cooking, cleaning, and baby-sitting. Often she has felt as if nobody really cared about her except her brothers and sisters, who treated her more like their mother than a sister.

When Janet was in seventh grade a new boy
came to her school. He was tall and handsome
and two years older than Janet. He had moved
several times and was left back. He paid attention
to Janet right away and made her feel wonderful.
On her thirteenth birthday he gave her a pretty
pearl ring and took her to a restaurant and then
they went dancing at an outdoor fair. Alex kept
telling her how beautiful she was and how he loved
her, and after much persuasion, she agreed she
would go to a secluded part of the beach at a nearby
lake, where they had intercourse. It seemed to
Janet that the only way she could make Alex keep
on loving her was to do what he wanted her to
do. The sex part was painful, and she was confused and shocked that it wasn't at all the way she
had thought it would be. At thirteen Janet got
pregnant. Alex was scared to death his parents
would find out. Janet's mother was very sad and
upset, but she helped Janet through her pregnancy until the fifth month when Janet had a mis-
carriage.

That was too much for a thirteen year old to
go through. Her life was already too hard; she had
grown up too fast. It was a terrible time except
for one thing; she realized that her mother did
love her a lot—she was just too tired and worried
and had had to give Janet too much responsibil-

ity. Janet had had to face a painful episode in her
life, and now that she is an adult, she knows she
was trying so hard to have somebody care about
her that she went through an experience that only
made her feel much worse.

Alex felt ashamed and guilty that he had run
away when Janet needed him, but later, when he
also was an adult, he realized that at fifteen he
was too young to take on such a serious responsi-
bility. It is because of such situations that your
parents worry about your teen years that lie just
ahead of you. The truth is that most adults are
not trying to be mean or overprotective when they
warn you against having sex too early; they worry
and warn because they so hope you will postpone
that good part of your life until you are mature
enough to understand that loving and responsibil-
ity and protection (of yourself as well as your part-
ner) all go together.

It is surely normal and natural to begin to have
sexual feelings as puberty begins, but what we do
about these feelings is terribly important. Both
boys and girls may begin to masturbate. Too often
this makes them feel ashamed and guilty. This is
a normal beginning to dealing with sexual feelings. There is no reason to feel ashamed of touch-
ing yourself and feeling pleasant sensations. The
only time that can become a problem is if it oc-

curs so often that it's almost the only thing a young person thinks about. Privately, alone, and occasionally, it is a natural release and a way to begin to understand the special feelings of being a boy or a girl.

Young people may also begin to experiment with kissing and hugging and holding; telling each other about secret feelings, wanting to be together, holding hands. This can become too serious too soon, unless you think carefully about what is happening. Parents and teachers and other adults who talk to you about postponing sexual relationships for a number of years are trying to help you get ready in every way, not just physically. This is now being brought home to you in a frightening and painful way. When I was young we were afraid of intercourse because the girl might get pregnant. Now there is still that danger, but there is also a far worse problem—AIDS, from which a person may die. If you were a lot older than you are it would be more natural for you to be cautious and careful. Being young, it is natural for you to be impulsive—not to think too clearly about the consequences of the things you do. That is why young people have more car accidents, take more chances with dangerous drugs—and are unprepared for the responsibilities of intimacy. It is natural for young people to think they are im-

mortal, that nothing terrible can happen. Being a
mature adult usually changes that feeling. By the
time you are in college or working you will be
able to think more clearly about the results of your
behavior.

I am sure you think your parents' ideas are old-
fashioned, that they come from the "Dark Ages."
That's how most young people feel about their
parents! But as you will someday discover for
yourself, sex relations with someone you love and
want to protect and take care of, and who feels
the same way about you, continues to be a lovely
experience that is worth waiting for and that each
person deserves.

There are some people who think the less you
know about your own bodies, about growing up
sexually, the better off you will be. I don't agree
at all. What I worry about is the misinformation
young people get about sex. The more you understand the facts and the feelings that are truthful,
the more you can use this information wisely.
The only thing I know to counteract the pornographic, titillating, seductive things you see and
hear is good sex education at home and in the
schools. Some people have the incorrect idea that
knowledge can harm you. This is only true if
the knowledge is making somebody rich by trying
to excite you. If grown men and women are drawn

to pornography, we cannot do anything about it, but the truth is that many of the adults who go to the "dirty movies" and who buy the "sexy magazines," or who read pornographic comics, are often people who did *not* get the necessary help they needed through sex education at an early age.

I hope many of you have programs in school where you can ask any question you want and where teachers talk to you as much about feelings as facts—where you don't have to be ashamed of ignorance or curiosity. But I know many of you don't have this opportunity. I hope you will try to help your parents understand that the more you know, the more you can make wise choices. If they feel very different, you might talk to your family doctor or an aunt or uncle, or a school nurse or a guidance counselor. When young people turn to pornography it may very well be because nobody is willing to talk about the normal feelings they are beginning to experience. I never met a young person who didn't feel confused and anxious about growing up sexually. Both boys and girls will do just about anything to keep this secret. You can be sure that most of the boasting in locker rooms and hallways is just whistling in the dark. Pretending can make a person feel more sure of him- or herself—at least for a few minutes. A teacher I know asked her seventh-grade English class to tell

her how they felt about boy–girl relationships. No
one said a word. Then she said they could write
anonymous compositions. They poured out their
hearts. She tried to help them understand that they
all had the same kinds of secret anxieties.

There are many ways in which equality between the sexes can lead to wonderful companion-
ship and sharing. This is especially true with falling
in love. It is no longer necessary for boys to boast
and girls to act as if they are shocked. Now they
can talk to each other as friends, share their worries and needs, not put on a big act of being very
confident and sophisticated.

There is one special part of sex that may upset
you a great deal because there is a normal, natural
stage in which young people may feel a genuine
attraction toward someone of their own sex. It is
common for girls to feel they love each other a
lot; they hug and kiss each other often. While
boys are a little more restrained, they are usually
not self-conscious about hugging each other after
a triumphant soccer game, or telling each other
their secrets, or preferring to spend time together
without any girls around. When puberty begins,
both boys and girls may become more self-conscious and uneasy about being affectionate or de-
monstrative with people of their own sex, even
though it may feel like a safer way to have a close

friendship. When I was in junior high school, I had two special girlfriends. We all loved poetry and the ballet; we wrote sad stories, and each of us kept a diary which nobody could see but the other two friends. We were, in a way, in love with each other. We learned a lot about loving feelings from each other.

Such feelings should not frighten you. It doesn't mean that you or your close friend of the same sex are going to become homosexuals. It is a normal stage in growing up. Often the person we love is an adult. When I was thirteen I was in love with a dramatics counselor at camp. I dreamt about her, I acted flirtatious, I wanted to show off for her. When she paid attention to me I was in heaven, when she seemed to like some other camper, I was jealous. What I was learning were important things about loving. I wanted to be an actress, so Irma and I had something in common. She had a lively sense of humor, and I wanted to be able to make people laugh too. And possibly most important of all, she introduced me to some writers who have remained important to me all my life. One was a book by Kahlil Gibran called *The Prophet* and fifty years later, it is still a book I read when I want to be inspired.

A special palship with another boy or with a man, another girl, another woman, is the way in which we experiment with our feelings, our goals for our own lives. It often feels easier and safer than being close friends with someone of the opposite sex. This phase usually passes as we gain confidence and become more and more interested in the opposite sex.

This is not true 100 percent of the time. Joel has had feelings which bother him very much, for a long time, even though he is only twelve. He has urges to touch other boys, to kiss them. He gets excited about being with a man. All his fantasies and dreams about sex have to do with other males. He has been so ashamed and frightened that he avoids having any close boy friends. He spends most of his time outside of school, alone. He tries everything he can think of to make these "bad thoughts" go away.

They are not bad thoughts. Joel is not a bad person, whether these feelings are temporary, or become much stronger. It is a possibility that Joel may be a homosexual, and he feels there is nothing he can imagine that would be worse than that. He is positive he could never tell his parents. The more he thinks he is some kind of crazy person, the more he may be in danger of doing something foolish, such as going to a place where there are homosexuals and having experiences which will terrify him; he could be abused and mistreated.

The need to mature and be a responsible person is the same for a homosexual as for a heterosexual. As in every other part of life, homosexuality all depends on what a person does about it. Just as in heterosexual relationships, some people are self-destructive, let others hurt them, or become so preoccupied with sex that nothing else in life seems important. And then there are people who behave with dignity and caring and know that what they really want is not passing infatuations but falling in love and having a permanent love relationship. Meanwhile they know that friendship is the way to move toward love.

There are many happy gay and lesbian couples, who stay "married" all of their adult lives. They are able to do this because they learned not to hate themselves for being different from most people. It is important for Joel to find someone to talk to. It is much easier now than it used to be. There are homosexuals who are psychologists and psychiatrists in many parts of the country. More nurses, doctors, and teachers undertand that homosexuality is not something a person chooses, but something someone is. Some communities have responsible and caring counseling groups. Eventually, it is to be hoped that Joel can tell his family. The biggest problem for homosexuals is the secrecy, the feeling of being abnormal and bad.

There are now support groups in many parts of
the country for the parents of homosexuals to help
them learn to accept the fact that their son or
daughter is still (and always was) a worthwhile
and lovable person and can have a valuable and
fulfilling life.

Boys and girls shouldn't come to the conclusion
that they are homosexual, even if there are strong
feelings for the same sex, until they are adults. I
don't believe that a person who remains strongly
attacted to people of the same sex should be forced
to try to change unless they want that more than
anything in the world. For such people, psycho-
therapy may help them to become heterosexual.
However, I believe it is better to be a homosexual
who is a decent, loving, thoughtful, caring happy
person, than to ruin one's life by feeling ashamed.

There is a great fear of homosexuality among
boys particularly. That is why you hear so many
"dirty jokes" about it, and why so many boys try
to be as macho as possible. It is slowly changing,
but we still live in a society that condemns homosexuality in many places, and among many
people. We still don't understand the causes of
homosexuality but more and more experts believe
it is a natural condition for some people.

If you worry about this matter, it might help
you to know that many gay people have made great

contributions to society. Some of the most macho athletes (football players, for example) are homosexuals. There are doctors, lawyers, and scientists who are homosexuals, not just ballet dancers and artists, as some people seem to think.

It is important not to make any decisions for quite awhile, and even more important is to understand that you are a person who wants affection, love, and understanding, just like anyone else, but that you may express these needs differently when you are an adult.

What may make it easier now for boys and girls to be friends is that you are learning much more about how to *talk* to each other about your feelings, and more parents and teachers are realizing how important it is to talk to you as well.

Growing up is not easy. But the most important thing you need to remember as you struggle through the adolescent years, is that you will gain in self-confidence and slowly but surely you will find out who you are and what you want to do with your life. Like every single person who ever grew up, you will make mistakes and feel you have failed and will never recover. But no matter what you do or what happens, you are always learning things you will need to understand as an adult.

Sometimes you will feel very much alone;

sometimes you will feel sad or confused, sometimes angry. Often you will feel frightened of your
feelings in relationships with boys and girls of your
own age. These are all normal feelings as you face
the adolescent years—which are the bridge to being grown up. Because of the hormonal and other
physical changes beginning to occur, these are, in
some ways, the most painful years, when being
an "in between" can be very upsetting. What you
need to remember is that it is also a time of moments of great joy and excitement, and that nothing in your life will ever be as important as loving,
caring relationships with other people, and that's
what you are studying right now.

6

Special Problems

By now you can surely tell that I do not agree with grownups who say, "Oh, childhood is such an easygoing, happy time!" On the contrary, not only are there the normal and expected mysteries and complications of growing up, but there are also lots of special problems, the kind that don't happen to every young person but do happen to enough of you so that it's important to talk about them.

For example, Sylvia has diabetes. She's now ten years old, and she has known she is a diabetic since she was six. Diabetes is an illness in which the body does not manage to deal properly with certain foods containing sugar, and when it is serious a person must avoid these foods very, very carefully and also have shots of insulin, a medication that helps the body function properly. The problem is that Sylvia is very self-conscious about being a diabetic and hates the idea of others in her school knowing about it. Sometimes in the cafeteria she will take a piece of cake or have an ice cream sundae, when she's with a group of friends, because she feels it's so important not to be different. Other times she "accidentally on purpose" may forget to give herself an insulin shot at the right time because she's embarrassed and ashamed and doesn't want anyone to see her.

Peter has what is called a clubfoot. It means he was born with a deformity of one foot, has already had several operations, and walks with a crutch quite often. He feels bitter and angry and hardly ever talks to anyone at school. He hates himself, thinks that he is being laughed at by everyone, and sometimes even wishes he'd never been born at all.

Sylvia and Peter have two kinds of problems. The first comes from inside themselves. Because there is something different about each of them, they think *everything* is wrong with them. This seems to be true in spite of the fact that their parents' attitudes have been quite different. Sylvia's parents acted as if it was the end of the world when they found out she had diabetes. Her mother cried, her father looked grim, when the doctor told them. The same night she heard her mother crying again in her parents' bedroom and talking about what a burden it was going to be to keep Sylvia on the right diet and to teach her to give herself shots of insulin several times a day. Her parents confirmed her fears that for the rest of her life she was going to be sick, and that nothing good would ever happen to her.

Peter's mother and father had always treated him as if nothing was really wrong with him. They kept telling him he could have a perfectly normal life, and while they were very sympathetic about the pain he endured after several operations, they refused to treat him like a cripple.

The reason Sylvia and Peter seem to have similar attitudes, in spite of their parents, is that being different in any way during their school years is a source of painful feelings. It is hard enough for adults to accept and adjust to any kind of disability; it is much, much harder during the years when kids want so much *not* to be different in any way.

The second part of the problem is that Sylvia and Peter are right; other kids *do* behave cruelly quite often. In third grade some of the kids on the school bus laughed and called Peter "Werewolf" when he had some difficulty getting up the steps on the bus. Several girls teased Sylvia by following her into the girl's bathroom, even climbing under the door of a stall, or climbing on a toilet and looking over the partition, when they knew she had gone into the bathroom to give herself an injection. After a few such experiences in the early grades, Sylvia and Peter have become unhappy loners. Whenever they see several kids talking together, they are sure the others are talking about them. When any boy or girl tries to be friendly, they feel sure it's only because the other person is curious and wants to find out more about their disabilities.

Young people with special differences need to understand as early as possible that a disability is not a description of a person—it is one part of a person with many, many other characteristics; not as simple as having blue or brown eyes or being tall or short, but also in no way the full story of a person. There are other things that are equally true. Sylvia dances beautifully, and the doctor has told her there is no reason she couldn't be a dancer as long as she sticks to her diet and takes her medication. She is also a person who loves children and is a wonderful baby-sitter to her younger brother. She is actually considered by others to be one of the prettiest girls in her class and several of her classmates would really like to be her friend.

But Sylvia doesn't trust them, cannot understand how other kids could be so mean, and so she spends most of her time alone, feeling she has to defend herself. What she needs to understand is that other children are actually scared of having anything wrong with them. There is an inaccurate but normal feeling that if you get too close to someone with a disability it might be catching! Fear is almost always behind any cruelty, as well as lack of information. The foolish idea is that if you make fun of someone who is different, the same thing can't happen to you. Just as Sylvia and Peter are miserable about being different in any way, so all their classmates dread any such possibility in themselves—and so Sylvia and Peter make them uneasy. Laughter, excluding a person, are ways of denying that anything like these problems can happen to oneself, and a way of defending oneself against feelings that are too painful.

Special problems need special attention from adults. The problems can very rarely be solved without help, although there are some young people who seem to take their disabilities in stride, and don't let these problems interfere with their lives. Most young people need some help.

When Sylvia's parents were told by the school nurse that Sylvia was "forgetting" to come for her medication, they talked to the doctor and she suggested that Sylvia might come once a week with a group of people her own age, all diabetics, who meet with a psychologist to talk about their feelings. Sometimes there can be great comfort and support in sharing common feelings, and out of such an experience a young person can learn to live more realistically and less destructively with special problems.

In fifth grade, Peter had a teacher who helped him face his problem openly. During the first week of school, Mr. Ortega noticed that Peter limped into the classroom in a very self-conscious way and always sat alone at the back of the room. After several weeks of watching Peter and seeing the reactions of others in the class, Mr. Ortega started out one morning by saying, "Good morning, class. Today we are not going to continue our discussion of the American Indian. Today we are going to have a special class in biology . . ." And continuing despite the shocked faces of Peter and everyone else, Mr. Ortega went on, "Everyone in this classroom knows that Peter has what is called a clubfoot. That happens to be one very small part of who Peter is, and we all better talk about it so we can stop thinking about it. Peter was born with a twisted foot. It is not something that can happen to anyone else in this class and it is certainly nothing that Peter can help. Once in a while a baby is born with a deformed foot, and while it is certainly too bad it is also not the end of the world. Peter can do almost anything he wants to do, except possibly be a baseball or football player." By this time, Peter was as red as a beet and the class looked shocked and was silent. Peter wanted to get up and punch Mr. Ortega and run out of the class and never come back.

Mr. Ortega went right on: "Now I want Peter to understand that I feel that the least important thing about him, in this classroom, is one of his feet. What I am interested in is Peter's composition on the Mohawk Indians. And what I am interested in is whether Peter and the rest of you can learn to solve math problems. And what I am most interested in is if you and Peter can begin to talk to each other and become friends and stop carrying on as if somebody in this classroom has leprosy. Is there anyone here who will tell me how they feel?" It took a few minutes but finally Bill stood up and said, "I invited Peter to my house but he wouldn't come." And then Virginia sort of whispered, "My mother has multiple sclerosis and has to be in a wheelchair, and I wondered if the same thing could happen to Peter." After a while others began to talk, and finally Mr. Ortega said, "Okay kids. That's the end of the biology lesson for today. Peter, I want you to cut out feeling so sorry for yourself—and the rest of you, I want you to think about the fact that no two people are ever exactly alike and you have to put up with that fact, even if it makes you uncomfortable. Louise, your skin is dark, like mine. Tom, you're the tallest in this class. Wah Chin, your eyes look different from mine. Clarise, your mother works nights, and you cook supper for your brothers and sisters. Lauri, you write the best poems in the class. Burt, you can't throw a ball to save your life. Ginny, you've got freckles. Pauline, your father is a Marine and isn't home a lot." By this time the kids in the class were laughing and looking a little shy, but their eyes were on Peter who was looking at the floor. Then Mr. Ortega said, "Okay, that's all. Peter, come on up and see me." After the others had left, Mr. Ortega said, "I know you're angry at me and you think everything will be worse, but it won't. I hope you will talk to me when you feel bad. But if you let them, you can have a lot of friends. I know you think your foot is *you,* but it isn't."

One sensitive and caring teacher, or one helpful support group isn't going to change everything overnight, but it is important for all young people, with or without special problems, to understand that the most serious disability anybody can have is thinking that being different is a terrible thing. The second-worst disability is not being able to *talk* about our feelings, to be honest with each other. When Peter can talk to a friend about how he feels, he will only have a clubfoot—he won't be disabled in other ways. When Sylvia can accept herself as a talented and lovely person, it won't be such a terrible hardship to take her injections; when she can even do this with a couple of friends watching her, then she will know diabetes is not an important way to describe her.

People who stutter worry constantly about being different, and the more they worry, the worse it gets. Sometimes young people can be very cruel by mimicking a stutterer. Another person in the class may be unusually heavy or another's ears may stick out a lot, or somebody else may have an unusually long nose. Each person needs to realize that whatever is special or different tells us practically nothing about the person. Each of us needs to see ourselves as made up of many parts, and each of us wants others to see us as total human beings, not just people who must deal with situations over which we have no control to change or remove.

Probably one of the hardest special problems to deal with is when a classmate is seriously ill. Roger has AIDS. He got it from a blood transfusion. He was only two when this happened; now he is twelve and often has to go to the hospital for chemotherapy treatments. He comes to school wearing dif-

ferent caps, but everyone knows the treatments
have made him bald. His oldest friends, since
kindergarten, seem to avoid him now. Roger is
deeply hurt. He doesn't understand that they care
so much about him, but they just cannot bear to
think of his suffering or dying. Some children avoid
Roger because they think they can catch AIDS
from him. Teachers, parents, doctors, need to explain this has *never* happened in ordinary everyday
contacts. Such a tragedy is almost more painful
than any person, child or adult, can bear, but it
is part of life, and sometimes there is no choice
but to bear it. It is easier on everyone if people
can share their feelings. The other thing that helps
us live through such painful experiences is taking
whatever action we can to help. Roger's closest
friends are encouraged to join their gym teacher
who says he's going to visit Roger in the hospital;
a teacher asks some other classmates to bring him
his homework; some others make him some funny
hats in art class. The unbearable becomes bearable
when we can talk about our fears and our painful
feelings, and when we do as much as we can to
help.

The other kinds of special problems have to do
with outside influences, things that happen to us
in groups, in neighborhoods, in the world we live
in. A major cause for your growing up faster today is that life is becoming more dangerous. When

I was growing up in New York City it was safe for me to travel alone, day or night. Although there surely were dangerous drugs being used in some places, I never even heard about them. Most streets were quiet and clean, and I was never afraid to travel in the subways. Now your parents and teachers feel they *must* discuss such things. There *are real* dangers, and not just in big cities.

In earlier years there were far fewer knives and guns involved in street fights due to drugs. Until quite recently, young people who lived on farms or in well-to-do suburbs felt safe from crime, but this is no longer true. Too many people, too many poor, too many growing up in unhappy families, too much child abuse, have created a much larger population of people who have very serious emotional problems, who hate themselves and are full of rage against a world that has gotten too complicated, frightening, and hostile, and so they lash out against others.

Katie was riding her bike home from school along a quiet country road when two boys jumped out of the bushes and told Katie to give them her bicycle. Without thinking, Katie got mad and tried to hold onto the bike, and one of the boys had a knife and cut her arm very badly. Katie should have been taught *never* to fight back, but to get away as quickly as possible.

Patrick's best friend in fifth grade told Patrick

it was fun to smoke marijuana and he was a nerd if he didn't try it. Patrick figured that his best friend couldn't possibly hurt him, so he tried some "grass." Gradually he got to like it, and then Simon told him he'd have to pay for it. Simon introduced him to Bruno who stayed about one block from the school and sold all kinds of drugs. After a few weeks Patrick couldn't seem to concentrate in school, and his grades went down. His allowance wasn't enough to keep buying marijuana, so he took some money from his mother's purse. Fortunately for Patrick his parents found out what was happening and were able to help Patrick stop what he was doing. But all young people need to learn about drugs both at home and in school, so that they understand the consequences of using drugs that can hurt their minds and force them to behave in dangerous ways. It is a shame to have to deal with such subjects, but there is no choice. There are dangerous people and dangerous neighborhoods. The bigger the population gets, the more disturbed people there are, and it is terribly important to learn how to protect yourself, to be able to say no, and to ask for adult help when you need it.

There is a girl in Roseanne's class who steals Roseanne's lunch money almost every day by threatening to beat her up. When Dennis started walking home after school, two men tried to give him some money and said they would give him "free crack" if he would sell it to some other kids. Caroline realizes she's the last to finish getting dressed in the gymnasium locker room and is suddenly in a panic about getting out of there, because there have been newspaper headlines about a person in the neighborhood who molests young girls.

You live in a frightening world. It influences your schoolwork and your friendships. Television, radio, and newspapers constantly warn you of dangers; your river is polluted, and it's not safe to fish there anymore; people are worrying about the water in their wells. So many countries have nuclear bombs, that the whole planet could be wiped out in a few minutes. When the weather changes in unusual ways, does it mean we have poisoned the atmosphere? Probably no children ever before had so many different kinds of fears. Not that life was ever 100 percent safe. A caveboy was afraid of the saber-toothed tiger! Children have always been afraid of things like smallpox and diphtheria, or of having to work in coal mines at the age of nine or ten. People throughout the ages have had every reason to fear earthquakes and volcanic eruptions.

But today's problems are different. For example, rather than having solved the problem of racial intolerance, there seems to be more conflict than ever before. My father used to tell me about the time when he was a young boy, an immigrant from Russia, when boys in the street would call him "kike" or "sheeny," and he'd run away. My husband made a mistake about school one day. He thought that after finishing some tests, he didn't have to go to school the following day. The principal (who was later fired for being a mentally ill and cruel person) punished the entire grade by making them stay after school for one week because "Larry had played hooky." Larry was beaten up on the way home from school every day and would go miles out of his way to escape his enemies if possible. Cruelty and fighting are surely not new, but serious and dangerous weapons are, and some children, afraid of what might happen to them, now have knives—even guns.

White people have insulted black people by calling them "niggers" and at one time or another, Irish people or Italians or Poles have been discriminated against in many jobs. Each new group coming to this country has had to struggle for equality and acceptance—black people most of all because they are the most easily identifiable.

Today, with a large immigration of Asians and Spanish-speaking people, there are new groups hating each other. This happens because we have become afraid of strangers, because we don't like people until we know them as individuals, and that's more and more difficult as the population (in classrooms and neighborhoods) increases.

The more frightening our communities become, the more likely it is that dangerous gangs will develop. Juan, a nineteen-year-old ex-convict, told me that by the time he was in third grade he knew he would "get killed on the way to school" if he didn't make himself a weapon and join the gang on his street. By the time he was ten, he had been in some terrible gang wars; by the time he was twelve, his gang had killed a boy from a rival gang.

The normal desire to be in a secret club, at a time when life was less threatening, has become something far more frightening and dangerous, and divides young people into hostile groups, each person labeled by the accident of his or her background—Italian, Jewish, Japanese, Vietnamese, Irish, black, Hispanic. The more we hear about crime and drugs, the more people become separated, never having the opportunity to get to know each other as fellow human beings, with the same feelings, the same needs, the same hopes. Serious community problems seem to force young people into attacking each other in groups instead of getting to know each other.

There are other special problems for young people, having to do with people who are mentally ill, both children and adults. In every such situation young people need to understand how important it is to tell adults about what is happening. Bruce, nine years old, teases the girls and sometimes gets one of them to go to some bushes near the school, where he wants to "play doctor" and pull down their pants and touch them in a special way; these girls need to tell someone. The reason they don't is because they think it's their fault and they are ashamed. It is *not* their fault, and Bruce needs help. The same thing is true when the science teacher, Mr. Matthews, tells Scott he wants to help him with a special project. He tells Scott he's the best student he's ever had, and he wants Scott to stay after school so they can work together. But Scott begins to feel very uncomfortable, because Mr. Matthews puts his arm around him all the time, and touches his leg when they are sitting at the desk working together. He suggests that Scott come to his apartment where they can work privately. Scott must tell an adult, not only for his own safety, but because Mr. Matthews is also a person who needs help with a serious emotional problem.

Once in a *very* great while a person is born with a mysterious mental problem that nobody understands too well. Most of you will never meet a child like the one I am going to describe, but because there may possibly be some danger to you if you do meet someone who is quite strange, I feel you should know about it. Let's say her name is Francine. She is ten years old. She is either in your school or is a neighbor. You can't figure out what is wrong but you get a queasy feeling in your stomach sometimes, or you may have bad dreams after being with her. She lies a lot and is very sneaky. The trouble is there is something about Francine that is very attractive—she kind of fascinates you. She wears strange combinations of clothes that make people give her a lot of attention. She tells weird stories about devils and strange ceremonies that she says are religious, but are really full of demons and cruel and dangerous ideas. She seems to have a great deal of power over you. You find that you want to try to please her, to be like her. She seems very self-confident, but she is acting all the time. Older children avoid her—she has no friends in her own age group, so she chooses younger children whom she feels can be more easily influenced to do what she tells them to do.

She makes you feel very excited, she flatters you, she gets you to do things you would not ordinarily do, such as lying to your parents, taking things that don't belong to you, or being mean to

other children. On the one hand you have a sort
of crush on her and on the other hand you are
afraid of her. Francine is the kind of person who
rarely gets hurt herself, but somehow she always
seems to be around when accidents happen to other
people. She encourages others to take dangerous
risks. Older children describe her as "weird," and
some part of you agrees, but another part of you
feels drawn to her.

This is not somebody who is just hurting in
their feelings and needs help from a counselor. In
fact, such people do not usually improve even when
they see a therapist regularly. Ordinarily they become more dangerous as they get older and may
break the law in any number of ways. Experts, in
trying to understand human behavior, call this kind
of person a "psychopath" or a "sociopath," which
means that they cannot help being the way they
are. They are never able to fully understand right
from wrong. They may be quite charming, but
they really cannot care for anyone else. They will
get away with just as much as they possibly can.

Before you decide you have met someone like
Francine, talk it over with your parents or your
teacher. As a matter of fact in most cases the adults
around you will already have noticed that *you* are
behaving strangely—that you have changed. In
most cases troubled children can be helped by being

treated with kindness and friendship. In the case of Francine, there is nothing you can do to help. What you need to do is never to play alone with someone like Francine—always have another child or grownup nearby, and when you feel you just cannot help doing something she wants you to do, you must ask for help. It is a very rare and unusual problem, but if you find yourself caught up in feelings and behavior that confuse and upset you when you are with another youngster, you really need to share this with an adult.

In the face of the kinds of special problems I've mentioned, what can you do? There are two important ingredients in answering that question which may sound like opposites, but really are not: caution and action. First of all, you need to decide that as much as you may want to be well liked, there are some people you must avoid at all cost. If you ever feel you are in serious danger you need to understand there is nothing wrong or weak about insisting on asking for the help of grown-ups. There are police officers to help to protect adults; you need teachers, parents, school guards, guidance counselors, and the police to protect you.

There is nothing shameful or cowardly about running away when you feel you are in danger of any kind. If you feel capable of it, you may want to learn something about boxing or the martial arts, so that you feel confident you might at least protect yourself against one other person. Being called a sissy or a coward is *not* the worst thing that can happen to you—being hurt is worse! Probably you have been taught that it is wrong to be a "tattletale." It is not wrong when you are in danger yourself or when you know that some bullies or dangerous gangs are in your school or neighborhood. Today young people cannot always, or even often, solve serious problems by themselves.

There are some things you can do to be careful and to protect yourself from becoming an "easy" victim:

1) It is foolish to carry more money than you actually need for the day.

2) Don't wear your best or most expensive clothes and jewelry to school, or bring radios or other valuable equipment to school.

3) Avoid as much as possible areas where gangs hang out—or if you must walk on these streets, ask an older and bigger relative or neighbor to walk with you or work out a buddy system with friends. If and when you sense real danger, tell your teacher or the school principal or a police officer.

4) Don't ever try to resist a robbery, give whatever is asked for and run.

5) Don't walk or ride a bicycle alone in deserted areas.

6) Never, ever, talk to anyone you don't know who offers you a ride home, or an ice cream cone, or anything else, even if this person says he or she knows your parents.

By now you may be feeling pretty depressed! But so far I have only been telling you half the story. Despite all these special problems, what you need to remember is that the large majority of people around you, both young people and adults, are kind, caring, sensible, responsible people. But it is important to recognize that there is a small but influential minority who can cause dangerous things to happen. It is important to feel there are things you and your family can do to change things that are wrong. Feeling helpless and at the mercy of a few unhappy, angry, even dangerous people can make a whole community feel terrible. Worrying about such problems as air and water pollution, homeless people, and toxic waste materials being dumped where there are homes and schools, begins to seem like an insurmountable mountain of troubles about which there is nothing one person or even a group of people can change. But neither you nor your families are helpless.

For one thing, you can help to raise money for groups that are trying to make the world a better place to live in. Kisha takes half of the money she earns baby-sitting and donates it to Greenpeace, one of the best organizations now dealing with problems of pollution. Justin asks people for money for UNICEF all year round, not just on Halloween. Ginger's fourth-grade class is planning a street fair in the playground of her school, to raise money for a neighborhood shelter for homeless families. They hope that the money will be used for toys and food for the children. There will be homemade cakes and cookies, aprons and smocks made in sewing classes, toys made in shop classes; games of skill will be made up by each class from kindergarten to sixth grade; special shows of dancing and singing are being planned by volunteers in each class, and there will even be a booth where people can have their fortunes told by the principal, Ms. Segal, dressed in a turban and a gypsy dress.

Eileen wrote a school assignment about all the junk that had been thrown in the nearby river, and her whole sixth-grade class started a campaign for a cleanup. First they went to see the editor of the local paper, who gave them a lot of publicity. Half the town turned out on a Saturday in June. They got the local sanitation department to send a truck, and in hip boots parents, teachers, church groups, school kids, and local politicians dragged rubber tires, old boxes, cans and bottles, and other garbage out of the river. The sixth graders made sandwiches and punch for all the volunteer workers.

In some schools, students and teachers have planned special assemblies to talk about racial and ethnic tensions. In one school they invited a parent who is a psychologist to talk about prejudice—why people in different groups look for a scapegoat to blame their problems on, why misunderstandings, even hatred, come from fear and frustration.

Abe's grandparents escaped from a concentration camp after World War Two. He decided that he would start an after-school club that anybody could join to talk about people of different backgrounds. Each member of the club would have a chance to tell the history of his or her family.

One thing we have learned is that *taking action* is the first step toward feeling less depressed and frightened. Imagine how proud you would feel if you were the person who went to your school principal and told him or her that there were some problems among the students and in the neighborhood that needed to be talked about, and that you were the person who started a community action program? What a great feeling! It isn't something that has to be done alone—a Scout group, a basketball team, an art class can be a place for sharing ideas and finding ways to deal with problems.

It is the serious problems which may very well be one of the first important ways in which you discover that being your own person is much more important than being like anyone else. It may be "cool" to try crack; but when you say no, you are saying, "I am beginning to like myself enough to want to take care of my life, not destroy it."

Each person has the power to make a difference. Sometimes it's by saying yes to volunteering one afternoon a week to play with children in a hospital, or going to talk to people in a senior citizen's group, or helping a Vietnamese student learn to read English. Often it is by saying no to a gang that beats up kids who walk through its "territory." It's saying no to anyone who offers you a drink or a drug.

When you say no to vandalism, or to taking any dangerous risks, you have finally reached a time when peer pressure is really not what life is all about.

Being able to help a fellow student who is shy

or lame or blind, being able to argue with fellow students who hate people for their color or their religion or their national background, and being able to interest others in working together, mean that you are developing your own values and can stand up for them. They are all ways of showing that you are growing up, and you can take a stand against things that are wrong. In this way problems become an opportunity for you to learn ways of handling them and, as a result, to feel proud of yourself.

7

Learning to Live Together

From the moment we are born we begin learning about living with other people. We smile, we snuggle, we cry—and with every human feeling and with all kinds of actions we begin to sense how other people react to us and how we react to other people. If we have brothers and sisters we begin to learn about mixed feelings—that you can love and hate a person at the same time. Conchita was four when Pablo was born; all of sudden she was no longer the center of attention. Why should she have to share her parents with this imposter? When Jennifer went to sleep-away camp, she got a postcard from her younger sister which was signed, "Love and Hate, Karen." You may have had a similar feeling—maybe a little loneliness for a brother or sister, but also quite a bit of pleasure in having more attention for yourself.

I remember a time when I couldn't stand even to look at my seven-year-old brother; he was such a slob and he always seemed to me to be dirty. One day, when I was about eleven, I came home from school and Richard was lying on his bed, all curled up. Nobody else was home. I asked him what was the matter and he told me he'd been bitten on his thigh by a dog. I raced to the phone, called the doctor, got my reserve allowance money for a taxi, and took him right to our doctor's office. I felt awful when he had to go for painful rabies injections for weeks and weeks. Sometimes anger is stronger, sometimes love is stronger. Whether you went to nursery school or learned first about relationships at home, by the time you were in kindergarten or first grade, you surely knew a great deal about how you felt about other people and how they felt about you.

What we all find out as we grow up is that human beings are a little like porcupines! If a porcupine is sitting in a cave on a cold winter night, it might wish for a little warmth and comfort from another porcupine—but if it finds a companion and tries to get very close, the other porcupine's quills might feel too sharp and scratchy. Human beings need and want to feel comforted and loved by other human beings, but sometimes we get annoyed and irritated, if someone comes too close.

All our lives we are learning ways to deal with contradictory feelings. We are also learning that we can't always have what we want when we want it. We learn to live with some feelings of frustration, and perhaps most important of all we learn that while there can never be anything wrong in acknowledging our feelings to ourselves, we can't always express what we feel in actions.

Keith feels very jealous of his new baby brother —the same feelings every first child has for a second child—but he is certainly not allowed to punch the baby or drown it in the bathtub! Barbara feels like killing her younger sister for damaging one of her most precious VCR tapes; she can yell at her but murder is out! By the time we get to school we have a pretty good idea about mixed emotions, and we are going to learn a great deal more about them.

Some of your parents and teachers may not agree with me, but I think that the most important thing you ever learn in school is about friendship. It is the basis of civilization. It is almost as important as food and air for living a good life. Enemies go to war; friends make peace. Friendship is an art, and when we learn about it during our school years, we can become much better human beings—and the world needs a lot of good people.

When you think about becoming an adult, or when you try to figure out the grownups around you, it may seem as if falling in love is just about the most important thing in most people's lives. The happy part like going to a wedding and seeing a bride and groom glowing with joy and confidence, or going to a movie in which men and women flirt with each other a lot, or the unhappy part which many of you know very well when parents fall out of love and divorce each other. We get the impression when we are children that love is what will make us blissfully happy or miserably unhappy.

That may well be true for many people who have never understood that all kinds of love— married love, parent love, child love—all depend on something much more important, and that is *friendship*. Grownups who stay happily married for forty or fifty years are people who learned how to be each other's very best friend as well as being in love. People who never get married may feel great love in their lives because they have good friends.

Friendship is a kind of loving that people have to work very hard to achieve. It is just about the best and most important thing that human beings are capable of—being a real friend and having real friends—and it takes years and years and years of growing up to learn the wonders and mysteries of friendship.

As you grow up you will probably have many acquaintances and a few very close friends. You will also have a few enemies—or at least people who don't like you. If you are going to have opinions and act on your beliefs, it is impossible to please everyone. But it is surely an important goal to try to get along with many people.

Learning how to be a friend helps us to discover which kinds of people we want to get to know better than other people. And when we figure out what it means to be a friend and have a friend, we begin to understand ourselves and to know how we want to live in the world with other people.

There are many different levels of relationships—some much better than others. Lenny is almost six feet tall in fifth grade. He's very powerful physically but not a very good student. Marco is quite short and is terrified of fighting and being hurt. Lenny threatens to beat up Marco unless he does his homework for him. That is *exploitation,* using another person for one's own gain.

Alison has been taught at home that black people are not as good as white people. There are two black girls in her sixth-grade class, Nicole and Maria. Alison doesn't fight with them or threaten them; she just ignores them and others in the class know that if you want to be Alison's friend you too must ignore Nicole and Maria. Alison isn't exploiting Nicole and Maria—she is sort of *tolerating* their existence. That can be almost as painful for them as being beaten up. And Alison may be missing out on a special friendship with either girl, because she hasn't allowed herself to get to know them.

Friendship is quite different. Let's suppose that Lenny went to Marco and said, "I need help. You're one of the best students in the class, and I just don't understand some of the things the teacher tells us." And suppose Marco would say, "I'll be glad to help you because you're the most important basketball player in school, and we all want you to pass your tests. And maybe you could help me not to be so afraid of team sports." And suppose Alison sat next to Nicole in the cafeteria and said, "My grandma lives in Alabama, and I heard your family used to live there." That might be the beginning of each girl understanding what it was like being black or white in Alabama in the past and now—an important history lesson for both girls. What I am describing is the best possible relationship between people—*mutual appreciation,* which means knowing that each of us grows and becomes more when we see good things in each other.

There is a catch to becoming a person who appreciates other people. The only way it can ever happen is if, first of all, we learn to appreciate ourselves. The main reason that Lenny and Marco were caught in a situation in which one person exploits another was that neither of them really felt good about themselves. Lenny felt stupid; Marco felt like a weakling. When, as in Alison's family, people feel they have to be superior to someone else or to a group of people, it is because somewhere, deep down, they feel inferior about something. It is literally impossible to appreciate anyone unless you appreciate yourself. And it isn't easy to feel self-confident when what you want most of all is to be like everyone else. This is what makes for so many difficulties in growing up, and there is no miracle, no recipe, for appreciating yourself. It is something I hope will happen to you by the time you are sixteen or seventeen, or maybe twenty, when being yourself becomes more important than being like anyone else. It is worth thinking about even before you can do it!

It takes all the years of growing up to figure out how to make friendships work. How can you deal with conflicts? How do you communicate with each other, make compromises? How can you negotiate differences without losing your own rights?

Ira keeps insisting that when he and Jed walk home from school, the shortest way is to cross a busy highway. Jed thinks that route is dangerous.

Can they reach any agreement? Could they compromise and take turns each day? I would say no, there can't be any compromise if one person sees a real danger in giving in. On the other hand if Ira wants to see one movie and Jed another, that might be something they can compromise about: one week Jed's choice, one week Ira's. I think the way we decide whether we can give in, accept another person's point of view, and work out equal sharing, depends on the subject. It's not an easy task but learning about friendship also means what you feel you can do and what you can't do. Jed may have to decide he will walk home alone—the safe way.

There is one kind of discrimination which is necessary and can sometimes even be a matter of life or death. Disliking a person without even knowing him or her, just because they belong to a certain race or religion, or are too rich or too poor, or because of some other characteristic which you see from the outside, is foolish and cruel. Foolish because you might miss out on a good friend and cruel because you are making a judgment which has nothing to do with the person inside. However, there are situations in which you must choose to have nothing to do with someone who has problems inside him- or herself and encourages you to hurt yourself or other people.

Becoming a friend and having friends is very

complicated—there are so many things to think about. Unfortunately, young people don't get much of a chance to spend time thinking about such things—they are too busy trying to keep up with schoolwork, which is more difficult today than it was when I was young. My neighbor, Fred, is in the fifth grade, and the other day he told me they were dissecting frogs in his class. I didn't have to do that until I was a high-school junior. His younger brother, Jim, showed me his fourth-grade math book, and I couldn't understand it at all. My granddaughter is being taught "cursive" writing in second grade. I wasn't taught that until fifth grade! I can't help wondering if she will be able to print when she grows up; it's a great help in addressing packages! There is more to learn, and most schools give quite a bit of homework (I had none until fifth grade), so that too little time is spent in school talking about feelings and learning more about each other.

Learning to become a civilized person seems to me to be just about the most important thing we need to learn. It means respecting others and caring about what happens to them. That can only happen when we begin to understand ourselves and know we are loveable and worthy human beings, and that can take much longer than learning grammar or American history or biology. It is something we have to work on all our lives.

Of course many parents and teachers care very deeply about how each one of you gets along with others. And there are practical ways in which adults and children can encourage "practice" in making friends. Class discussions about family experiences, such as vacation trips, can help us learn about each other. Some schools now have counselors who come into the school and have special meetings with children whose parents have been divorced, so that there can be a genuine sharing of feelings and mutual sympathy and encouragement. Some teachers like to have the children in their classes write compositions or diaries, without having to put their names on them, so the class can talk about personal feelings without revealing who wrote what. Any time a class goes on a trip, chances are that while having a good time and feeling relaxed, and having a common adventure, classmates will get to know each other in new ways. Many teachers realize that when two or three children can work together on a project they are likely to learn as much about each other as the subject they are studying.

Parents, grandparents, other relatives, and neighbors can also help a great deal to enhance and encourage friendships. Inviting friends to visit you at home is probably the most important way for young people to get to know each other better. Caroline wrote a composition entitled, "How I Got

to Know My Friend." It was about a girl she had
hardly ever noticed in class. She wrote, "I never
even talked to Stacey—she was very quiet and sat
in the back of the room. I really couldn't remember whether I ever saw her talking to anyone. One
day she came up to me and asked if I would come
to her house for lunch on Saturday. I started to
say no, but I could see it was very hard for her to
ask me, so I said yes. Boy, was I surprised when
I got there! The walls of the house were covered
with paintings and drawings! Stacey was a terrific
artist, and I don't think anyone in school knew
it. I think it took a lot of courage to invite me,
because I could see Stacey was shy. [Some people
seem to be born more shy and quiet, just as some
people are born outgoing and active.] But Stacey
knew I had a lot of friends, and I think she wanted
me to tell other people about her being an artist.
When she began to talk about painters and art
museums, she stopped being quite so shy, and I
liked her a lot. And what she told me was interesting. I am going to go to a museum with her
next Saturday."

One of the best ways to turn enemies into friends
is inviting someone who picks on you or teases
you to come to a family barbecue or go on a day's
fishing trip with you and your mother or father.
Alexis was having a hard time getting to know

other girls in her class after she moved and changed schools. Her mother suggested she invite a few girls she liked to a pajama party. Things were a little cool and distant at first, and a number of girls turned Alexis down before she was able to get four girls to come, but it was a great success. Her father had them help him make his favorite fancy chocolate fudge cake, cleverly figuring out how to have five bowls to lick, and her mother helped the girls make up some funny skits. She provided makeup and costumes and took pictures for each girl to take home in a little album of her own.

There is one way to develop a friendship that I have to admit most parents can't stand! It drove me crazy when my daughter was growing up, but I tried to remember how great it was when I was young—talking on the telephone! If grownups ask you why you can spend an hour talking to someone you saw all day in school, you can try to explain it to them! You might ask them how they felt when they were your age.

What happens is that when you are young you can feel very shy and awkward talking to someone your own age about your feelings, your dreams and hopes, your fears. Face-to-face you feel self-conscious and uneasy. But when you and a friend are just voices on a phone, and you don't have to

look at each other, you can have a much more
intimate conversation. Hopefully as each of us
grows and becomes more sure of ourselves—and
has had a chance to express feelings over the telephone—we are able to share just as well face-to-
face. But even adults sometimes feel the same way
as you do, that they can speak more freely on the
phone.

One of the most difficult things to figure out is
how to be a caring person who has compassion for
someone else and still be sure you care about
yourself as well. Joanne has a real problem. Shuko
is a Vietnamese refugee. She and her family were
so relieved and grateful to come to the United
States, but they live in a neighborhood where there
is a lot of prejudice against Asians. What has happened is that the poor people who lived there first
feel they are being crowded out by the newcom-
ers, that they are taking away jobs, that their ways
are too different, that too many live in one apartment. Joanne happens to be a very caring person,
and she feels sorry for Shuko. When she begins to
stick up for Shuko and invites her to her house,
Shuko is very grateful and begins to cling to
Joanne. She wants to spend all her time, in school
and out, with Joanne. She follows her everywhere,
and Joanne begins to realize she has no time for
her other friends and that she is falling behind

on her homework assignments. How can she tell Shuko she can't spend so much time with her?

Derek has spent most of his time alone. He is bored in school. He hasn't been able to find anyone in his class who is as smart as he is or interested in the things that interest him. His teachers decided that he should be skipped two full grades because he was a genius, and even then he would probably be ahead of the class academically, but they worried about his social development—how could a twelve-year-old make friends with children who were fourteen or fifteen? There would be such a difference in maturity. But Derek met a boy named Nathan who wanted to be a physicist, and they could talk about Einstein and quantum mechanics and go to lectures that were open to the public at a nearby college. The problem was that Nathan was unhappy about not being as mature socially as the fourteen-year-olds in his class and wanted help; he didn't want to spend all his time with Derek who was perfectly happy having someone to talk to about intellectual subjects. Nathan's family wanted him to join a club, a young people's group at their temple, and go to school dances. How could Nathan let Derek know he wanted to do things without Derek?

When we feel as if someone is taking too much of our time and yet we care about the other per-

son's feelings, it is important to take action, not
to sacrifice one's own needs. In many cases you
need the help of other people. Joanne needs to let
the teachers know how needful Shuko and her
family are. Maybe Shuko's mother and father could
come and tell about their wartime experiences in
Vietnam and how they came to America after many
years in a refugee camp. Maybe the school principal and the guidance counselor can alert other
groups in the community about what is happening in Shuko's neighborhood. Maybe Joanne knows
a minister she could talk to about helping Asians
in the community to be more warmly welcomed,
and about how there must be social agencies that
could be of more help to the whole neighborhood.
Sometimes calling a radio or TV program that is
interested in community affairs might bring attention to a problem. Joanne can begin to intro-
duce Shuko to more of her friends and perhaps
have a special party in Shuko's honor so she can
begin to feel comfortable with others.

Nathan may have to try to solve his problem
on his own. He may have to tell Derek quite openly
and honestly that he feels they are spending too
much time together, and while he does certainly
enjoy being with Derek, he needs time for other
things. It needn't be a question of one extreme or
the other—they can still spend some time to-

gether, but not as much, not because he likes Derek any less, but because both of them need to have experiences with others.

There is a very special good feeling when friends stick up for each other. Whether a friend is wrong or right, the feeling that you will love them and defend them to others no matter what is one way of knowing you are really a friend or that someone is surely your friend. We don't always have to approve of everything someone we love does, but one of the most precious things is giving and getting unconditional love. That means that you care so much about another person that no matter what they do, you will go right on caring about them. I'm sure you know what a good and special feeling it is when someone feels that way about you. This is again one of the hardest things to do during the early school years, when being accepted and being like everyone else seems so important. Later on when a person feels good enough about him- or herself to enjoy being an individual, it becomes easier to give unconditional love. Many young people are lucky enough to learn about this special kind of loving from their grandparents!

When Oliver was ten years old, he felt sad much of the time because he didn't have a "best friend." At the beginning of fifth grade he met a boy who had recently moved to his neighborhood and was new to the school. Ross could tell that Oliver was looking for a friend, and since Ross felt unsure of himself, he figured that Oliver might be the person to become friends with first, and then, later on, when he began to feel more comfortable and people didn't view him as a stranger, he could get to know other kids in his class. The two boys became inseparable, and somewhat to the surprise of each of them, they began to care a great deal about each other.

After a few months Oliver told Ross something he rarely mentioned and didn't want to talk about to just anyone. His biological father had not been married to his mother—both birth parents had been high school students—and Oliver had been adopted by his present family. Oliver was sure that Ross was such a good close friend he would never tell anyone.

But then Ross began to have very strong feelings of attraction to a girl in one of his classes. Yvonne was very pretty and one of the most popular girls in the fifth grade. Ross wanted to make an impression on Yvonne, and when he told her he knew a secret about another student she became more interested in him. Ross told her Oliver's secret, and soon everyone knew about it. When we are young and want more than anything to be popular, we may betray one friend to gain another. The person who does this always regrets it and feels guilty. But it is very hard to control the impulse to become more popular. It may help to control such impulses if we can remember it never really works; sooner or later the person we are trying to win over realizes we aren't to be trusted. It never becomes easy to be a loyal friend who can keep confidences, but it is something to hope we will be able to do more often as we grow up.

Another thing that makes it hard to learn about friendships is that there is no way of knowing how things are going to turn out. I mentioned in an earlier chapter a girl named Phyllis and how jealous and envious I was of her in second grade. For over fifty years she has been my closest friend! I could never have imagined that the most popular and beautiful girl would ever pay attention to me! In high school we wrote poetry and went to concerts and read books about psychology. Now we help each other through every sad event and rejoice when good things happen. Nothing could ever come between us; we understand each other, and most of all, we love each other no matter what our mistakes may be, and we want the other one to use her talents, have a rich and full life. Each of us has failed sometimes, but that only brings us closer. Long, long ago, she told me that she too felt shy and clumsy when she was very young.

I was amazed, but I learned that even the people we think are perfect don't always feel that way about themselves.

Once when I went to give a speech in Chicago, from the airport I called another girl, Jane, whom I thought was the smartest person in the school and I wished I was just like her. We had a long talk on the phone. I discovered we had absolutely nothing in common, disagreed totally about politics. She was a full-time housewife, so the fact that she always got the highest grades on tests apparently hadn't made her the president of some college like Harvard!

At school reunions from time to time, the boys on whom I'd had crushes—Stewart, Carl, and Walter—thought I was really somebody, and much to my surprise I came to realize that while I spent most of elementary school and the beginning of high school sure I would never amount to anything, it turned out that I was one of the most successful people in my class, and had accomplished wonderful things after all.

There is no way in which you can predict the future. Your worst enemy could become your best friend next year. Someone you think could become President of the United States, because he or she is so brilliant and popular, may turn out to be a person you never hear about again. You may think that you will never learn enough math to get into college or get a good job. People who doubted themselves in elementary school, just like you, become congressmen and congresswomen, judges, social workers, writers—just about anything they want to be once they are old enough to realize what they want to do.

Most of all, there is no way you can tell now who your dearest friends will be, how many close friends you will have, what falling in love as an adult will be like. All these aspects of friendship sound very heavy and serious. The truth is that having friends is *fun*! The giving and receiving of compassion, affection, loyalty, and understanding can lead to lots of joking and laughing and joy.

The most important thing to be doing right now is taking chances, taking risks, not worrying all the time if you are going to succeed or fail as you try to make friends with different people. Right now is the time for trial and error. There is no way you can grow up knowing who you really are unless you are willing to experiment. Not everyone is going to like you, no matter what you do. Not every friendship is going to be helpful in your growing up. Fortunately, no matter how you and your peers try, you will *not* grow up to all be alike. What a boring world that would be! The main thing is that you are all growing up at the same time, together, and every time you have a new friendship you are learning more and more about what kind of person you like and likes you and what kind of person you want to be. Slowly but surely all of you will hopefully learn to *appreciate each other,* and that is the most important thing that ever can happen.

EDA LESHAN has been an educator and family counselor for many years. Well-known also as author, columnist, and television host, she has written over twenty books, including *Learning to Say Goodbye: When a Parent Dies* (Macmillan), *What's Going to Happen to Me: When Parents Separate and Divorce* (Four Winds), and *When Grownups Drive You Crazy* (Macmillan). In addition Mrs. LeShan has appeared as a guest on such programs as *Good Morning America, The Today Show,* the *Donahue* show, and many others.

Mrs. LeShan has received numerous awards for her work, including the Karl Menninger Award from the Fortune Society, the Distinguished Alumnus Award from Teacher's College, Columbia University, and the Mothers of America Award. Mrs. LeShan lives with her husband in New York City. Her daughter Wendy and granddaughter Rhiannon live in Massachusetts.